A TOUCH OF INFINITY

A TOUCH
OF INFINITY

Thirteen New Stories
of Fantasy and
Science Fiction

by HOWARD FAST

William Morrow & Company, Inc., New York 1973

I. T

PRINTED IN THE UNITED STATES OF AMERICA.

LIBRARY OF CONGRESS CATALOG CARD NUMBER 72-135

ISBN 0-688-00180-7

For Bill Segal

who opened the door

Contents

A TOUCH OF INFINITY

1

The Hoop

In one of those charming expressions of candor—which were to become so well known to the television audience —Dr. Hepplemeyer ascribed his scientific success less to his brilliance than to his name. "Can you imagine being Julius Hepplemeyer, and facing that for the rest of your life? If one is Julius Hepplemeyer, one is forced either to transcend it or perish."

Two Nobel Prizes before he finally perfected the hoop attested to the transcendence. In acknowledging them, he made liberal use of what the press came to call "Hepplemeyer Jewels," as for instance: "Wisdom obligates a man to perform foolishly." "Education imposes a search for ignorance." "The solution always calls for the problem."

This last was particularly applicable to the hoop. It was never Dr. Hepplemeyer's intention to bend space, and he pinned down the notion as presumptuous. "Only God bends space," he emphasized. "Man can merely watch, observe, seek—and sometimes find."

"Do you believe in God?" a reporter asked eagerly.

"In an ironic God, yes. The proof is laughter. A smile is the only expression of eternity."

He talked that way without any particular effort, and acute observers realized it was because he thought that way. His wife was an acute observer, and one morning at breakfast, as he cracked a three-minute egg and peered into it, he explained that everything returns to itself.

It rather chilled his wife, without her knowing why. "Even God?" she asked.

"Most certainly God," he replied, and for the next two years he worked on the hoop. The Dean at Columbia co-operated with him, cutting down his lectures to one a week. Every facility was placed at his disposal. After all, it was the Hepplemeyer age; Einstein was dead, and Hepplemeyer had to remind his admirers that while "Hepplemeyer's Law of Return" had perhaps opened new doors in physics, it nevertheless rested solidly upon the basis of Einstein's work. Yet his modest reminders fell upon deaf ears, and whereas *The New York Times* weekly magazine supplement once ran no less than six features a year on some aspect of Einstein's work, they now reduced the number to three and devoted no less than seven features in as many months to Hepplemeyer. Isaac Asimov, that persistent unraveler of the mysteries of science, devoted six thousand words toward a popular explanation of the "Law of Return," and if few understood, it was never-theless table conversation for many thousands of intrigued readers. Nor were any egos bruised, for Asimov himself estimated that only a dozen people in the entire world actually understood the Hepplemeyer equations.

Hepplemeyer, meanwhile, was so absorbed in his work that he ceased even to read about himself. The lights in his laboratory burned all night long while, with the help of his eager young assistants—more disciples than paid workers– he translated his mathematics into a hoop of shining aluminum, the pipe six inches in diameter, the hoop itself a circle of the six-inch aluminum pipe twelve feet in diameter, and within the six-inch pipe, an intricate coil of gossamer wires. As he told his students, he was in effect building a net in which he would perhaps trap a tiny curl of the endless convolutions of space.

Of course, he immediately denied his images. "We are so limited," he explained. "The universe is filled with endless wonders for which we have no name, no words, no concepts. The hoop? That is different. The hoop is an object, as anyone can see."

There came a fine, sunny, shining day in April, when the hoop was finally finished, and when the professor and his student assistants bore it triumphantly out onto the campus. It took eight stalwart young men to carry the great hoop, and eight more to carry the iron frame in which it would rest. The press was there, television, about four thousand students, about four hundred cops, and various other representatives of the normal and abnormal life of New York City. The Columbia University quadrangle was indeed so crowded that the police had to clear a path for the hoop. Hepplemeyer begged them to keep the crowd back, since it might be dangerous; and as he hated violence almost as much as he detested stupidity, he begged the students not to get into the kind of rumble that was almost inevitable when cops and students were too many and in too great proximity.

One of the policemen lent the professor a bullhorn, and he declared, in booming electronic tones, "This is only a test. It is almost impossible that it should work. I have calculated that out of any given hundred acres, possibly a hundred square feet will be receptive. So you see how great the odds are against us. You must give us room. You must let us move about."

The students were not only loose and good-natured and full of grass and other congenial substances on that shining April day; they also adored Hepplemeyer as a sort of Bob Dylan of the scientific world. So they cooperated, and finally the professor found a spot that suited him, and the hoop was set up.

Hepplemeyer observed it thoughtfully for a moment and then began going through his pockets for an object. He found a large gray eraser and tossed it into the hoop. It passed through and fell to the ground on the other side.

The student body—as well as the working press—had no idea of what was supposed to happen to the eraser, but the crestfallen expression on Hepplemeyer's face demonstrated that whatever was supposed to happen had not happened. The students broke into sympathetic and supportive applause, and Hepplemeyer, warming to their love, took them into his confidence and said into the bullhorn:

"We try again, no?"

The sixteen stalwart young men lifted hoop and frame and carried their burden to another part of the quadrangle. The crowd followed with the respect and appreciation of a championship golf audience, and the television camera ground away. Once again, the professor repeated his experiment, this time tossing an old pipe through the hoop. As with the eraser, the pipe fell to earth on the other side of the hoop.

"So we try again," he confided into the bullhorn. "Maybe we never find it. Maybe the whole thing is for nothing. Once science was a nice and predictable mechanical handmaiden. Today two and two add up maybe to infinity. Anyway, it was a comfortable old pipe and I am glad I have it back."

By now it had become evident to most of the onlookers that whatever was cast into the hoop was not intended to emerge from the other side, and were it anyone but Hepplemeyer doing the casting, the crowd, cameras, newsmen, cops and all would have dispersed in disgust. But it was Hepplemeyer, and instead of dispersing in disgust, their enchantment with the project simply increased.

Another place in the quadrangle was chosen, and the hoop was set up. This time Dr. Hepplemeyer selected from his pocket a fountain pen, given to him by the Academy, and inscribed *"Nil desperandum."* Perhaps with full consciousness of the inscription, he flung the pen through the hoop, and instead of falling to the ground on the other side of the hoop, it disappeared. Just like that—just so—it disappeared.

A great silence for a long moment or two, and then one of Hepplemeyer's assistants, young Peabody, took the screwdriver, which he had used to help set up the hoop, and flung it through the hoop. It disappeared. Young Brumberg followed suit with his hammer. It disappeared. Wrench. Clamp. Pliers. All disappeared.

The demonstration was sufficient. A great shout of applause and triumph went up from Morningside Heights and echoed and reechoed from Broadway to St. Nicholas Avenue, and then the contagion set in. A coed began it by scaling her copy of the poetry of e.e. cummings through the hoop. It disappeared. Then enough books to stock a small library. They all disappeared. Then shoes—a veritable rain of shoes—then belts, sweaters, shirts, anything and everything that was at hand was flung through the hoop, and anything and everything that was flung through the hoop disappeared.

Vainly did Professor Hepplemeyer attempt to halt the stream of objects through the hoop; even his bullhorn could not be heard above the shouts and laughter of the delighted students, who now had witnessed the collapse of basic reality along with all the other verities and virtues that previous generations had observed. Vainly did Professor Hepplemeyer warn them.

And then, out of the crowd and into history, raced Ernest Silverman, high jumper and honor student and citizen of Philadelphia.

In all the exuberance and thoughtlessness of youth, he flung himself through the hoop—and disappeared. And in a twinkling, the laughter, the shouts, the exuberance turned into a cold, dismal silence. Like the children who followed the pied piper, Ernest Silverman was gone with all the fancies and hopes; the sun clouded over, and a chill wind blew.

A few bold kids wanted to follow, but Hepplemeyer barred their way and warned them back, pleading through the bullhorn for them to realize the danger involved. As for Silverman, Hepplemeyer could only repeat what he told the police, after the hoop had been roped off, placed under a twenty-four-hour guard, and forbidden to everyone.

"But where is he?" summed up the questions.

"I don't know," summed up the answer.

The questions and answers were the same at Centre Street as at the local precinct, but such was the position of Hepplemeyer that the Commissioner himself took him into his private office—it was midnight by then—and asked him gently, pleadingly:

"What is on the other side of that hoop, Professor?"

"I don't know."

"So you say—so you have said. You made the hoop."

"We build dynamos. Do we know how they work? We make electricity. Do we know what it is?"

"Do we?"

"No, we do not."

"Which is all well and good. Silverman's parents are

here from Philadelphia, and they've brought a Philadelphia lawyer with them and maybe sixteen Philadelphia reporters, and they all want to know where the kid is to
the tune of God knows how many lawsuits and injunc-
tions."

Hepplemeyer sighed. "I also want to know where he is."

"What do we do?" the Commissioner begged him.

"I don't know. Do you think you ought to arrest me?"

"I would need a charge. Negligence, manslaughter, kid-
napping—none of them appear to fit the situation exactly,
do they?"

"I am not a policeman," Hepplemeyer said. "In any
case, it would interfere with my work."

"Is the boy alive?"

"I don't know."

"Can you answer one question?" the Commissioner
asked with some exasperation. "What is on the other side
of the hoop?"

"In a manner of speaking, the campus. In another
manner of speaking, something else."

"What?"

"Another part of space. A different time sequence.
Eternity. Even Brooklyn. I just don't know."

"Not Brooklyn. Not even Staten Island. The kid would
have turned up by now. It's damn peculiar that you put
the thing together and now you can't tell me what it's
supposed to do."

"I know what it's supposed to do," Hepplemeyer said
apologetically. "It's supposed to bend space."

"Does it?"

"Probably."

"I have four policemen who are willing to go through
the hoop—volunteers. Would you agree?"

"No."

"Why?"

"Space is a peculiar thing, or perhaps not a thing at all," the professor replied, with the difficulty a scientist always has when he attempts to verbalize an abstraction to the satisfaction of a layman. "Space is not something we understand."

"We've been to the moon."

"Exactly. It's an uncomfortable place. Suppose the boy is on the moon."

"Is he?"

"I don't know. He could be on Mars. Or he could be a million miles short of Mars. I would not want to subject four policemen to that."

So with the simple ingeniousness or ingenuousness of a people who love animals, they put a dog through the loop. It disappeared.

For the next few weeks, a police guard was placed around the hoop day and night, while the professor spent most of his days in court and most of his evenings with his lawyers. He found time, however, to meet with the mayor three times.

New York City was blessed with a mayor whose problems were almost matched by his personality, his wit, and imagination. If Professor Hepplemeyer dreamed of space and infinity, the Mayor dreamed as consistently of ecology, garbage, and finances. Thus it is not to be wondered at that the Mayor came up with a notion that promised to change history.

"We try it with a single garbage truck," the Mayor begged Hepplemeyer. "If it works, it might mean a third Nobel Prize."

"I don't want another Nobel Prize. I didn't deserve the first two. My guilts are sufficient."

"I can persuade the Board of Estimate to pay the damages on the Silverman case."

"Poor boy—will the Board of Estimate take care of my guilt?"

"It will make you a millionaire."

"The last thing I want to be."

"It's your obligation to mankind," the Mayor insisted.

"The college will never permit it."

"I can fix it with Columbia," the Mayor said.

"It's obscene," Hepplemeyer said desperately. And then he surrendered, and the following day a loaded garbage truck backed up across the campus to the hoop.

It does not take much to make a happening in Fun City, and since it is also asserted that there is nothing so potent as an idea whose time has come, the Mayor's brilliant notion spread through the city like wildfire. Not only were the network cameras there, not only the local and national press, not only ten or twelve thousand students and other curious city folk, but also the kind of international press that usually turns out only for major international events. Which this was, for certainly the talent for producing garbage was generic to mankind and perhaps the major function of mankind, as G.B.S. had once indelicately remarked; and certainly the disposal of the said garbage was a problem all mankind shared.

So the cameras whirred, and fifty million eyes were glued to television screens as the big Sanitation truck backed into position. As a historical note, we remember that Ralph Vecchio was the driver and Tony Andamano his assistant. Andamano stood in the iris of history, so to speak, directing Vecchio calmly and efficiently:

"Come back, Ralphy—a little more—just cut it a little. Nice and easy. Come back. Come back. You got another twelve, fourteen inches. Slow—great. Hold it there. All right."

Professor Hepplemeyer stood by the Mayor, muttering under his breath as the dumping mechanism reared the great body back on its haunches—and then the garbage began to pour through the hoop. Not a sound was heard from the crowd as the first flood of garbage poured through the hoop; but then, when the garbage disappeared into infinity or Mars or space or another galaxy, such a shout of triumph went up as was eminently proper to the salvation of the human race.

Heroes were made that day. The Mayor was a hero. Tony Andamano was a hero. Ralph Vecchio was a hero. But above all, Professor Hepplemeyer, whose fame was matched only by his gloom, was a hero. How to list his honors? By a special act of Congress, the Congressional Medal of Ecology was created; Hepplemeyer got it. He was made a Kentucky Colonel and an honorary citizen of Japan and Great Britain. Japan immediately offered him ten million dollars for a single hoop, an overall contract of a billion dollars for one hundred hoops. Honorary degrees came from sixteen universities, and the city of Chicago upped Japan's offer to twelve million dollars for a single hoop. With this, the bidding between and among the cities of the United States became frantic, with Detroit topping the list with an offer of one hundred million dollars for the first—or second, to put it properly—hoop constructed by Hepplemeyer. Germany asked for the principle, not the hoop, only the principle behind it, and for this they were ready to pay half a billion marks, gently reminding the professor that the mark was generally preferred to the dollar.

At breakfast, Hepplemeyer's wife reminded him that the dentist's bill was due, twelve hundred dollars for his new brace.

"We only have seven hundred and twenty-two dollars in the bank." The professor sighed. "Perhaps we should take a loan."

"No, no. No indeed. You are putting me on," his wife said.

The professor, a quarter of a century behind in his slang, observed her with some bewilderment.

"The German offer," she said. "You don't even have to build the wretched thing. All they want is the principle."

"I have often wondered whether it is not ignorance after all but rather devotion to the principle of duality that is responsible for mankind's aggravation."

"What?"

"Duality."

"Do you like the eggs? I got them at the Pioneer super-market. They're seven cents cheaper, grade A."

"Very good," the professor said.

"What on earth is duality?"

"Everything—the way we think. Good and bad. Right and wrong. Black and white. My shirt, your shirt. My country, your country. It's the way we think. We never think of one, of a whole, of a unit. The universe is outside of us. It never occurs to us that we are it."

"I don't truly follow you," his wife replied patiently, "but does that mean you're not going to build any more hoops?"

"I'm not sure."

"Which means you are sure."

"No, it only means that I am not sure. I have to think about it."

His wife rose from the table, and the professor asked her where she was going.

"I'm not sure. I'm either going to have a migraine head-ache or jump out of the window. I have to think about it too."

The only one who was absolutely and unswervingly sure of himself was the Mayor of New York City. For eight years he had been dealing with unsolvable problems, and there was no group in the city, whether a trade union, neighborhood organization, consumers' group, or Boy Scout troop which had not selected him as the whipping boy. At long last his seared back showed some signs of healing, and his dedication to the hoop was such that he would have armed his citizenry and thrown up barricades if anyone attempted to touch it or interfere with it. Police stood shoulder to shoulder around it, and morning, evening, noon, and night an endless procession of garbage trucks backed across the Columbia College quadrangle to the hoop, emptying their garbage.

So much for the moment. But the lights burned late in the offices of the City Planners as they sat over their drawing boards and blueprints, working out a system for all sewers to empty into the hoop. It was a high moment indeed, not blighted one iota by the pleas of the mayors of Yonkers, Jersey City, and Hackensack to get into the act.

The Mayor stood firm. There was not one hour in the twenty-four hours of any given day, not one minute in the sixty minutes that comprise an hour, when a garbage truck was not backing up to the hoop and discharging its cargo. Tony Andamano, appointed to the position of inspector, had a permanent position at the hoop, with a staff of assistants to see that the garbage was properly discharged into infinity.

Of course, it was only to be expected that there would be a mounting pressure, first local, then nationwide, then worldwide, for the hoop to be taken apart and minutely reproduced. The Japanese, so long expert at reproducing and improving anything the West put together, were the first to introduce that motion into the United Nations, and they were followed by half a hundred other nations. But the Mayor had already had his quiet talk with Hepplemeyer, more or less as follows, if Hepplemeyer's memoirs are to be trusted:

"I want it straight and simple, Professor. If they take it apart, can they reproduce it?"

"No."

"Why not?"

"Because they don't know the mathematics. It's not an automobile transmission, not at all."

"Naturally. Is there any chance that they can reproduce it?"

"Who knows?"

"I presume that you do," the Mayor said. "Could you reproduce it?"

"I made it."

"Will you?"

"Perhaps. I have been thinking about it."

"It's a month now."

"I think slowly," the professor said.

Whereupon the Mayor issued his historic statement, namely: "Any attempt to interfere with the operation of the hoop will be considered as a basic attack upon the constitutional property rights of the City of New York, and will be resisted with every device, legal and otherwise, that the city has at its disposal."

The commentators immediately launched into a discussion of what the Mayor meant by otherwise, while the Governor, never beloved of the Mayor, filed suit in the Federal Court in behalf of all the municipalities of New York State. NASA, meanwhile, scoffing at the suggestion that there were scientific secrets unsolvable, turned its vast battery of electronic brains onto the problem; and the Russians predicted that they would have their own hoop within sixty days. Only the Chinese appeared to chuckle with amusement, since most of their garbage was recycled into an organic mulch and they were too poor and too

thrifty to be overconcerned with the problem. But the
Chinese were too far away for their chuckles to mollify
Americans, and the tide of anger rose day by day. From
hero and eccentric, Professor Hepplemeyer was fast becoming scientific public enemy number one. He was now
publicly accused of being a Communist, a madman, an
egomaniac, and a murderer to boot.

"It is uncomfortable," Hepplemeyer admitted to his
wife; since he eschewed press conferences and television
appearances, his admissions and anxieties usually took
place over the breakfast table.

"I have known for thirty years how stubborn you are.
Now, at least, the whole world knows."

"No, it's not stubbornness. As I said, it's a matter of
duality."

"Everyone else thinks it's a matter of garbage. You still
haven't paid the dentist bill. It's four months overdue now.
Dr. Steinman is suing us."

"Come, now. Dentists don't sue."

"He says that potentially you are the richest man on
earth, and that justifies his suit."

The professor was scribbling on his napkin. "Remark-
able," he said. "Do you know how much garbage they've
poured into the hoop already?"

"Do you know that you could have a royalty on every
pound? A lawyer called today who wants to represent—"

"Over a million tons," he interrupted. "Imagine, over a
million tons of garbage. What wonderful creatures we are!
For centuries philosophers sought a teleological explanation for mankind, and it never occurred to any of them
that we are garbage makers, no more, no less."

"He mentioned a royalty of five cents a ton."

"Over a million tons," the professor said thoughtfully.
"I wonder where it is."

It was three weeks later to the day, at five-twenty in the morning, that the first crack appeared in the asphalt paving of Wall Street. It was the sort of ragged fissure that is not uncommon in the miles of city streets, nothing to arouse notice, much less alarm, except that in this case it was not static. Between five-twenty and eight-twenty, it doubled in length, and the asphalt lips of the street had parted a full inch. The escaping smell caught the notice of the crowds hurrying to work, and word went around that there was a gas leak.

By ten o'clock, the Con Edison trucks were on the scene, checking the major valves, and by eleven, the police had roped off the street, and the lips of the crack, which now extended across the entire street, were at least eight inches apart. There was talk of an earthquake, yet when contacted, Fordham University reported that the seismograph showed nothing unusual—oh, perhaps some very slight tremors, but nothing unusual enough to be called an earthquake.

When the streets filled for the noon lunch break, a very distinct and rancid smell filled the narrow cavern, so heavy and unpleasant that half a dozen more sensitive stomachs upchucked; and by one o'clock, the lips of the crack were over a foot wide, water mains had broken, and Con Edison had to cut its high-voltage lines. At two-ten, the first garbage appeared.

The first garbage just oozed out of the cut, but within the hour the break was three feet wide, buildings had begun to slip and show cracks and shower bricks, and the garbage was pouring into Wall Street like lava from an erupting volcano. The offices closed, the office workers fled, brokers, bankers, and secretaries alike wading through the garbage. In spite of all the efforts of the police and the fire department, in spite of the heroic rescues of the police helicopter teams, eight people were lost in the garbage or trapped in one of the buildings; and by five o'clock the garbage was ten stories high in Wall Street and pouring into Broadway at one end and onto the East River Drive at the other. Now, like a primal volcano, the dams burst, and for an hour the garbage fell on lower Manhattan as once the ashes had fallen on Pompeii.

And then it was over, very quickly, very suddenly—all of it so sudden that the Mayor never left his office at all, but sat staring through the window at the carpet of garbage that surrounded City Hall.

He picked up the telephone and found that it still worked. He dialed his personal line, and across the mountain of garbage the electrical impulses flickered and the telephone rang in Professor Hepplemeyer's study.

"Hepplemeyer here," the professor said.

"The Mayor."

"Oh, yes. I heard. I'm terribly sorry. Has it stopped?"

"It appears to have stopped," the Mayor said.

"Ernest Silverman?"

"No sign of him," the Mayor said.

"Well, it was thoughtful of you to call me."

"There's all that garbage."

"About two million tons?" the professor asked gently.

"Give or take some. Do you suppose you could move the hoop—"

The professor replaced the phone and went into the kitchen, where his wife was putting together a beef stew. She asked who had called.

"The Mayor."

"Oh?"

"He wants the hoop moved."

"I think it's thoughtful of him to consult you."

"Oh, yes—yes, indeed," Professor Hepplemeyer said. "But I'll have to think about it."

"I suppose you will," she said with resignation.

2
The Price

Frank Blunt himself told the story of how, at the age of seven, he bought off a larger, older boy who had threatened to beat him up. The larger boy, interviewed many years later, had some trouble recalling the incident, but he said that it seemed to him, if his memory was at all dependable, that Frank Blunt had beaten up his five-year-old sister and had appropriated a bar of candy in her possession. Frank Blunt's second cousin, Lucy, offered the acid comment that the dollar which bought off the larger boy had been appropriated from Frank's mother's purse; and three more men whose memories had been jogged offered the information that Frank had covered his investment by selling protection to the smallest kids at twenty-five cents a kid. Be that as it may; it was a long time ago. The important factor was that it illustrated those two qualities which contributed so much to Frank Blunt's subsequent success: his gift for appropriation and his ability to make a deal if the price was right.

The story that he got out of secondary school by pur-
chasing the answers to the final exam is probably apoc-
ryphal and concocted out of spleen. No one ever accused
Frank Blunt of being stupid. This account is probably
vestigial from the fact that he bought his way out of an
expulsion from college by paying off the dean with a cool
two thousand dollars, no mean sum in those days. As with
so many of the stories about Frank Blunt, the facts are
hard to come by, and the nastiest of the many rumors per-
taining to the incident is that Frank had established a
profitable business as a pimp, taking his cut of the earn-
ings of half a dozen unhappy young women whom he had
skillfully directed into the oldest profession. Another
rumor held that he had set up a mechanism for obtaining tests in advance of the testing date and peddling them
very profitably. But this too could not be proved, and all
that was actually known was his purchase of the dean. It
is also a matter of record that when he finally left college
in his junior year—a matter of choice—he had a nest egg
of about fifty thousand dollars. This was in 1916. A year
later he bought his way out of the draft for World War I
in circumstances that still remain obscure.

Two years later he bought State Senator Hiram Gillard
for an unspecified price, and was thereby able to place
four contracts for public works with kickbacks that netted
him the tidy sum of half a million dollars—very nice
money indeed in 1919. In 1920, when Frank Blunt was
twenty-four years old, he purchased four city councilmen
and levied his service charge on fourteen million dollars'
worth of sewer construction. His kickback amounted to a
cool million dollars.

By 1930 he was said to be worth ten million dollars,
but it was the beginning of a muckraking period and he
was swept up in the big public utility scandals and in-

dicted on four counts of bribery and seven of fraud. Frank Blunt was never one to count small change, and at least half of his ten-million-dollar fortune went into the purchase of two federal judges, three prosecutors, five assistant prosecutors, two congressmen, and one juryman—on the basis that if you are going to fix a jury, it's pointless to buy more than one good man.

One of the congressmen subsequently became a business associate, and Frank Blunt moved out of the scandal with clean hands and the receivership of three excellent utility companies, out of which he netted sufficient profit to more than replace his expenses for the cleansing.

He often said, afterward, that his Washington contacts made during that time were worth more than the expenses he incurred in, as he euphemistically put it, clearing his name; and unquestionably they were, for he got in at the rock bottom of the offshore oil development, operating with the boldness and verve that had already made him something of a legend in the financial world. This time he purchased the governor of a state, and it was now that he was said to have made his famous remark:

"You can buy the devil himself if the price is right."

Frank Blunt never quibbled over the price. "You cast your bread upon the waters," he was fond of saying, and if he wanted something, he never let the cost stand in his way. He had discovered that no matter what he paid for something he desired, his superb instinct for investment covered him and served him.

Politicians were not the only goods that Frank Blunt acquired. He was a tall, strong, good-looking man, with a fine head of hair and commanding blue eyes, and he never had difficulties with women. But while they were ready to line up and jump through his hoop free of cost, he preferred to purchase what he used. These purchases were temporary; not until he was forty-one years old and worth upward of fifty million dollars did he buy a permanent fixture. She was a current Miss America, and he bought her not only a great mansion on a hill in Dallas, Texas, but also four movies for her to star in. Along that path, he bought six of the most important film critics in America, for he was never one to take action without hedging his bets.

All of the above is of another era; for by the time Frank Blunt was fifty-six years old, in 1952, he was worth more money than anyone cared to compute; he had purchased a new image for himself via the most brilliant firm of public relations men in America; and he had purchased an ambassadorship to one of the leading western European countries. His cup was full, and it runneth over, so to speak, and then he had his first heart attack.

Four years later, at the age of sixty, he had his second heart attack; and lying in his bed, the first day out of the oygen tent, he fixed his cold blue eyes on the heart specialist he had imported from Switzerland—who was flanked on either side by several American colleagues—and asked:

"Well, Doc, what's the verdict?"

"You are going to recover, Mr. Blunt. You are on the road."

"And just what the hell does that mean?"

"It is meaning that in a few weeks you will be out of the bed."

"Why don't you come to the point? How long have I got to live after this one?" He had always had the reputation of being as good as his name.

The Swiss doctor hemmed and hawed until Blunt threw him out of the room. Then he faced the American doctors and specified that there was no one among the four of them who had collected less than twenty thousand in fees from him.

"And none of you will ever see a red cent of mine again unless I get the truth. How long?"

The consensus of opinion was a year, give or take a month or two.

"Surgery?"

"No, sir. Not in your case. In your case it is contra-indicated."

"Treatment?"

"None that is more than a sop."

"Then there is no hope?"

"Only a miracle, Mr. Blunt."

Frank Blunt's eyes narrowed thoughtfully, and for a few minutes he lay in bed silent, staring at the four uncomfortable physicians. Then he said to them:

"Out! Get out, the whole lot of you."

Five weeks later, Frank Blunt, disdaining a helping hand from wife or butler, walked out of his house and got into his custom-built twenty-two-thousand-dollar sports car, whipped together for him by General Motors—he was a deeply patriotic man and would not have a foreign car in his garage—told his chauffeur to go soak his head, and drove off without a word to anyone.

Blunt was not a churchgoer—except for weddings and funerals—but his flakmade image described him as a religious man whose religion was personal and fervent, and the wide spectrum of his charities included a number of church organizations. He had been baptized in the Baptist church, and now he drove directly to the nearest Baptist church and used the knocker of the adjacent parsonage. The Reverend Harris, an elderly white-haired and mild-mannered man, answered the door himself, surprised and rather flustered by this unexpected, famous, and very rich caller.

"I had heard you were sick," he said lamely, not knowing what else to say.

"I'm better. Can I come in?"

"Please do. Please come in and sit down. I'll have Mrs. Harris make some tea."

"I'll have some bourbon whiskey, neat."

Pastor Harris explained unhappily that bourbon whiskey was not part of his household but that he had some sherry that was a gift from one of his parishioners.

"I'll have the tea," said Frank Blunt.

The pastor led Blunt into his study, and a very nervous and excited Mrs. Harris brought tea and cookies. Blunt sat silently in the shabby little study, staring at the shelves of old books, until Mrs. Harris had withdrawn, and then he said bluntly, as befitting his name and nature:

"About God."

"Yes, Mr. Blunt?"

"Understand me, I'm a businessman. I want facts, not fancies. Do you believe in God?"

"That's a strange question to ask me."

"Yes or no, sir. I don't make small talk."

"Yes," the pastor replied weakly.

"Completely?"

"Yes."

"No doubts?"

"No, Mr. Blunt. I have no doubts."

"Have you ever seen Him?"

"Seen who?" the pastor asked with some bewilderment.

"God."

"That's a very strange question, sir."

"All my questions are strange questions. My being here is a damn strange thing. If you can't answer a question, say so."

"Then let me ask you, sir," said Pastor Harris, his indignation overcoming his awe, "do you believe in God?"

"I have no choice. I'll repeat my question. Have you ever seen Him?"

"As I see you?"

"Naturally. How else?"

"In my heart, Mr. Blunt," Harris said quietly, with curious dignity. "Only in my heart, sir."

"In your heart?"

"In my heart, sir."

"Then, damn it, you don't see Him at all. You believe something exists—and where is it? In your heart. That's no answer. That's no answer at all. When I look into my heart, I see two damn coronaries, and that's all."

"The more's the pity for that," Pastor Harris thought, and waited for Frank Blunt to come to the point of his visit.

"Joe Jerico sees Him," Blunt said, almost to himself.

Harris stared at him.

"Joe Jerico!" Blunt snapped.

"The revivalist?"

"Exactly. Is he a man of God or isn't he?"

"That's not for me to say," Harris replied mildly. "He does his work, I do mine. He talks to thousands. I talk to a handful."

"He talks to God, doesn't he?"

"Yes, he talks to God."

Frank Blunt rose and thrust out his hand at the old man. "Thank you for your time, Parson. I'll send you a check in the morning."

"That's not necessary."

"By my lights it is. I consulted you in a field where you're knowledgeable. My doctor gets a thousand dollars for a half hour of his time. You're worth at least as much."

The following afternoon, flying from Dallas, Texas, to Nashville, Tennessee, in his private twin-engine Cessna, Frank Blunt asked his pilot the same question he had asked Harris the day before.

"I'm a Methodist," replied Alf Jones, the pilot.

"You could be a goddamn Muslim. I asked you something else."

"The wife takes care of that," said Alf Jones. "My goodness, Mr. Blunt, if that was on my mind, flying around from city to city the way I do, I'd sure as hell turn into a mother-loving monk, wouldn't I?"

A chauffeur-driven limousine was waiting at the airport—not a hired car; Blunt kept chauffeur-driven custom-built jobs at every major airport—and the chauffeur, after a warm but respectful greeting, sped the car around the city toward that great, open, two-hundred-acre pasture that had been named "Repentance City."

"You're looking well, Mr. Blunt, if I may say so," the chauffeur remarked.

"What do you know about Joe Jerico?" Blunt asked him.

"He's a fine man."

"What makes you say so?"

"Take my old grandaddy. He was the dirtiest, sinfulest old lecher that ever tried to rape a nice little black girl. Truth is, we couldn't have a woman near him. That is, when he wasn't drunk. When he was drunk, he was just a mean and dangerous old devil and he'd just as soon break a bottle of corn over your head as say hello."

"What the hell has that got to do with Joe Jerico?"

"He went to one gathering—just one—and he saw the light."

"How is he now?"

"Saintly. Just so damn saintly you want to crack him across the head with a piece of cordwood."

"One meeting?"

"Yes, sir, Mr. Blunt. One meeting and he got the word."

It was dark when they reached Repentance City, but batteries of giant floods turned the vast parking area into

daylight. Thousands of cars were already there, like a sea
of beetles around the vast, looming white tent. Blunt respected size and organization. "How many does the tent
hold?" he asked his chauffeur.

"Ten thousand."

"He fills it?"

"Every night. You wouldn't believe it, Mr. Blunt, but
they drive two, three hundred miles to be here. He has a
loudspeaker setup, and sometimes he has an overflow
of two, three thousand can't get into the tent. So they sit
in their cars, just like a drive-in movie."

"Admission?"

"Just two bits. He won't turn away the poor, but then
he takes up a collection."

They parked, and Blunt then told the chauffeur to wait,
while he made his way on foot to the tent. There must
have been two or three hundred ushers, men and women,
organizing the crowd and handing out leaflets and song
sheets, the men in white suits, the women in white dresses.
It was an enormous, businesslike, and well-conducted operation, and some quick arithmetic told Blunt that the
nightly take, out of admission and nominal contributions,
should approach a minimum of five thousand dollars. By
his standards it was not tremendous, but it marked Joe
Jerico as very much a man of practical affairs, however
metaphysical his profession might be.

Blunt paid his quarter, entered, and found himself a
seat on a bench toward the rear, sandwiched between a
very fat middle-aged old woman and a very lean old man.
Already the tent was almost filled to capacity, with only
a rare space to be seen here and there; just a few minutes
after he arrived, the meeting started with a choir of fifty
voices singing "Onward, Christian Soldiers." A second and
a third hymn followed, and then the house lights went

down and a battery of spots fixed on stage center. The backdrop was a black cyclorama, the curtain of which parted for Joe Jerico to step into the spotlights, not a tall man, not a short man, straight, wide-shouldered, with a big head, a great mane of graying hair, and pale gray eyes like bits of glowing ice.

No introduction; he plunged right in with a voice that had the timbre of an organ: "My text is St. John, eight, twelve. 'Then spake Jesus unto them, saying, I am the light of the world: he that followeth me shall not walk in darkness, but shall have the light of life.' Do you believe? So help me God, I hope not. This is no place for believers. This is for the unbelievers, for the lost, for the misbegotten, for the devil-pursued, for the lost, I say, for you come in here and you come home and you are found! Open your hearts to me . . ."

Frank Blunt listened, intent and thoughtful, less touched by emotion than by admiration for the man's masterly command of the crowd. He played them as one plays a great instrument, as if indeed he was the extension of some mighty force that operated through him. His voice, naturally deep and full timbred, magnified by the public address system, touched with just sufficient trace of a southern accent, battered his audience, grabbed them, held them and used them.

Frank Blunt observed. He listened as the charge of emotion built up; he nodded with appreciation as the sinners went forward to be saved at the urgent, pleading command of Joe Jerico, and he admired the smoothness and the fine organization of the collection, just at the right moment of emotional completion. He ignored the slotted box as it went down his row, and accepted the hostile glances of those beside him. He sat and watched thoughtfully, and when it was over and the emotionally filled crowd, so many of them in tears, filed out, he re-

mained seated. He remained seated until he was the last
person in the huge tent, and then an usher approached
him and asked whether he was all right.

"My name is Frank Blunt," he said to the usher. "Here
is my card. I want to see Mr. Jerico."

"Mr. Jerico sees no one now. He is understandably
fatigued. Perhaps—"

"I'm here now and I wish to see Mr. Jerico. Take him
my card. I'll wait here."

Frank Blunt was not easy to resist. He had issued orders
for so many years and had been obeyed for so many years
that people did his will. The usher took the card, walked
the length of the tent, disappeared for a few minutes, re-
appeared, walked the length of the tent, and said to Blunt:

"Reverend Jerico will see you. Follow me."

Back through the tent, through the black curtain, and
then backstage past the curious glances of the ushers,
the choir singers, and the rest of the large staff Joe
Jerico carried with him; and then to the door of a large,
portable dressing room. The usher knocked at the door.
The deep voice of Jerico answered, "Come in." The usher
opened the door and Frank Blunt entered the dressing
room. The room was an eight-by-fourteen trailer; it had
taste, it had class, and it had Joe Jerico in a green silk
dressing gown, sipping at a tall glass of orange juice.

Blunt measured it with a quick glance, as he did the
man. There was nothing cheap or modest about Joe
Jerico; his work was no work that Blunt had ever encountered before, but the tycoon liked the way he did it.

"So you're Frank Blunt." Jerico nodded at a chair. "Sit
down. Tomato juice, orange juice—we have no hard
liquor—I can give you some wine."

"I'm all right."

No handshake, neither warmth nor coolness, but two
men eyeing each other and measuring each other.

"I'm glad you made it this time," Joe Jerico said finally.

"Why?"

"Because it gives you time for repentance."

"I didn't come here for repentance."

"Oh?" Jerico's eyes narrowed. "What then?"

"The doctors give me a year. They're liars. It's in the nature of the profession. If they gave me less, they figure I'd fire them."

"What do you give yourself?"

"Three to six months."

"Then I'd say you need repentance, Mr. Blunt."

"No, sir. I need life, Mr. Jerico."

"Oh? And how do you propose to go about that?"

"What do you know about me, Mr. Jerico?"

"What's on the record, more or less."

"Let me fill in then. I began my career by buying a college dean. I found that if the price is right, you can buy—and there are no exceptions. I have bought judges, city councilmen, district attorneys, jurors, congressmen, and senators. I bought the governors of two states. I have bought men and women and thoroughbred horses. I took a fancy to a princess once, and I bought a night in bed with her. It cost me twenty-five thousand dollars. I bought the dictator of a European country and I once had occasion to buy a member of the Central Committee of the Communist Party of the Soviet Union. He cost less than the princess, but he was more profitable in the long run."

He said all this, never taking his eyes from Jerico's face. Jerico listened with interest.

"You're a forthright man, Mr. Blunt."

"I don't have time to crap around, Mr. Jerico."

"What do you propose?"

"I like you, Mr. Jerico. You see the point and you come to it. I want to live. I propose to buy off God."

Jerico nodded, his pale eyes fixed on Blunt. He remained silent, and Frank Blunt waited. Minutes of silence passed, and still Frank Blunt waited patiently. He respected a man who considered a proposition carefully.

"You're not dealing with the principal. You're dealing with an agent," Jerico said finally. "How do you propose to enforce the contract?"

"I'm not an unreasonable man. I'm sixty years old. I want fifteen years more. I've made arrangements with a man whose line of work is the enforcing of contracts. If I die before the fifteen years are up, he will kill you."

"That's sound," Jerico agreed after a moment. "I like the way you think, Mr. Blunt."

"I like the way you think, Mr. Jerico."

"Then perhaps we can do business."

"Good. Now what's your price?"

"How much are you worth, Mr. Blunt?"

"About five hundred million dollars."

"Then that's the price, Mr. Blunt."

"You're not serious?"

"Deadly serious."

"Then you're insane."

Jerico smiled and spread his hands. "What's the alternative, Mr. Blunt? I could suggest the reward that awaits a man who has lived well—but no one takes any money with him to that place. You want it here on earth."

"To hell with you!" Blunt snorted. But he didn't get up. He sat there, watching Jerico.

"I didn't come to you," Jerico said softly. "You came to me."

Silence again. The silence dragged on, and this time Jerico waited patiently. Finally Blunt asked:

"How much will you let me keep?"

"Nothing."

"A man doesn't live on air and water. A million would see me through."

"Nothing."

"Well, I've heard it said that I have more money than God. Now it's reversed. The fact is, Mr. Jerico, that you drive a hard bargain, a damn hard bargain. I don't need money; I have a credit line of twenty million. You have a deal. Suppose we let the lawyers get together tomorrow."

It took seven weeks for the lawyers to finish the legal arrangements and for the papers to be signed. On the eighth week, Frank Blunt suffered a stroke. He was taken to the Dallas Colonial Nursing Home, which Joe Jerico immediately purchased, installing his own staff of doctors, nurses, and technicians. A year later Frank Blunt was still alive. A mechanical heart had taken over the function of his own weary instrument; a kidney machine flushed his body; and nourishment was fed to him intravenously. Whether or not he was more than a vegetable is difficult to say, but the report issued by Joe Jerico, who visited him once a week, was that he lived by faith—a testimony to faith.

By the third year, Joe Jerico's weekly visits had ceased. For one thing, his home was in Luxembourg—re the tax benefits—and his fortune was increasing at so lively a pace that he abhorred the thought of airplanes. He found his eighteen-thousand-ton yacht sufficient for his travel needs. His revivals had decreased to one a year, but whenever he was in America for the occasion, he made certain to visit Frank Blunt.

Frank Blunt died in 1971—fifteen years to the day from the time in Joe Jerico's dressing room when they had shaken hands and closed their deal. Actually his death was caused by a malfunction of the artificial heart, but it was only to be expected. So much had happened; the world had forgotten Frank Blunt.

Joe Jerico received the word on his yacht, which was lying in the harbor at Ischia, where he had come to spend a few days at the Duke of Genneset's villa, and he was late to dinner because he thoughtfully took the time to compose a message of condolence to Blunt's family. Jerico, at fifty, was still a fine figure of a man, comfortable indeed, but he had by no means lost his faith. As he told the young woman who accompanied him to dinner:

"God works in strange ways."

3
A Matter of Size

Mrs. Herbert Cooke—Abigail Cooke—was a woman with a social conscience and a sense of justice. She came of five generations of New Englanders, all of whom had possessed social consciences and devotion to justice, qualities not uncommon in New England once the burning of witches was gotten over with. She lived in a lovely old Colonial house on fifteen acres of land in Redding, Connecticut; she forbade any spraying of her trees, and she gardened ecologically. She believed firmly in mulch, organic fertilizers, and the validity of the New Left; and while she herself lived quietly with her teen-age children—her husband practiced law in Danbury—her heart and small checks went out to a multitude of good causes. She was an attractive woman, still under forty, an occasional Congregationalist, and a firm advocate of civil rights. She was not given to hysterics.

She sat on her back porch—unscreened—on a fine summer morning and shelled peas and saw something move. Afterward she said that it appeared to be a fly, and she picked up a flyswatter and swatted it. It stuck to the fly-swatter, and she looked at it carefully; and then she began to have what amounted to hysterics, took hold of herself, thanked heaven that her children were at day camp, and, still unable to control her sobbing, telephoned her husband.

"I've killed a man," she said to him.

"You what? Now wait a minute," he replied. "Get hold of yourself. Are you all right?"

"I'm all right."

"Are the children all right?"

"They're at day camp."

"Good. Good. You're sure you're all right?"

"Yes. I'm a little hysterical—"

"Did I hear you say that you killed a man?"

"Yes. Oh, my God—yes."

"Now please get hold of yourself, do you hear me, Abby? I want you to get hold of yourself and tell me exactly what happened."

"I can't."

"Who is this man you think you killed? A prowler?"

"No."

"Did you call the police?"

"No. I can't."

"Why not? Abby, are you all right? We don't have a gun. How on earth could you kill someone?"

"Please—please come home. Now. Please."

In half an hour Herbert Cooke pulled into his driveway, leaped out of his car, and embraced his still shivering wife. "Now, what's all this?" he demanded.

She shook her head dumbly, took him by the hand, led him to the back porch, and pointed to the flyswatter.

"It's a flyswatter," he said impatiently. "Abby, what on earth has gotten into you?"

"Will you look at it closely, please?" she begged him, beginning to sob again.

"Stop crying! Stop it!"

Convinced by now that his wife was having some kind of a nervous breakdown, he decided to humor her, and he picked up the flyswatter and stared at it. He stared at it for a long, long moment, and then he whispered, "Oh, my God—of all the damn things!" And then, still staring, he said to her, "Abby, dear, there's a magnifying glass in the top drawer of my desk. Please bring it to me."

She went into the house and came back with the magnifying glass. "Don't ask me to look," she said.

Herbert placed the flyswatter carefully on the table and held the magnifying glass over it. "My God," he whispered, "my God almighty. I'll be damned. A white man, too."

"What difference does that make?"

"No difference—none at all. Only—my God, Abby, he's only half an inch tall. I mean if he were standing up. Perfectly formed, the blow didn't squash him, hair, head, features—naked as the day he was born—"

"Must you carry on like that? I've killed him. Isn't that enough?"

"Honey, get a grip on yourself."

"I thought it was a fly. I saw it out of the corner of my eye. I saw it and swatted it. I'm going to throw up."

"Stop that. You didn't kill a human being. A human being isn't half an inch tall."

"I'm going to throw up."

She raced into the house, and Herbert Cooke continued to study the tiny object under the magnifying glass. "Of all the damn things," he muttered. "It's a man all right,

five fingers, five toes, good features, blond hair—handsome
little devil. I can imagine what the flyswatter felt like, like
being trapped under one of those iron blasting mats.
Squashed him a bit—"

Pale, but more in command of herself, Abigail returned
to the porch and said, "Are you still looking at that dreadful thing?"

"It's not a dreadful thing, Abby."

"Can't you get rid of it?"

Herbert raised his head from the magnifying glass and
stared at his wife thoughtfully. "You don't mean that,
Abby."

"I do."

"Abby, this is the strangest damn thing that ever happened to us, possibly to anyone. I mean, there simply is
no such thing as a human being half an inch tall."

"Except on that flyswatter."

"Exactly. We can't just throw him away. Who is he?"

"What is he?"

"Exactly," Herbert agreed. "What is he? Where did he
come from? Or where did it come from? I think you
understand my point," he said patiently and gently.

"What is your point?" she asked, a note of coldness
coming into her voice.

"I'm a lawyer, Abby. I'm an officer of the court. That's
my life, that's not something I forget."

"And I'm your wife, which is something you appear to
have forgotten."

"Not at all. You have done nothing wrong. Nothing. I
will stake my legal life on that."

"Go on."

"But we have a body here. It's only half an inch long,
but it's still a body. We have to call the police."

"Why? It's done. I killed the poor thing. I have to live
with that. Isn't that enough?"

"My dear, let's not be dramatic. We don't know what it is. You swatted an insect. For all we know, it is some kind of an insect."

"Let me look through that magnifying glass."

"Are you sure you want to?"

"I'm perfectly all right now."

He handed her the magnifying glass, and she peered through it. "It's not an insect," she said.

"No."

"What will the children say? You know how they are— when you wanted to put out poison for the rabbits that were eating the lettuce."

"The children don't have to know anything about it. I'll call Chief Bradley. He owes me a favor."

Herbert and Bradley sat in the chief's office and stared at the flyswatter. "Couldn't bring myself to take it off the flyswatter," Herbert said. "But I forgot to bring the magnifying glass."

The chief slowly and deliberately took a magnifying glass from his desk drawer and held it over the flyswatter. "I'll be damned," he murmured. "Never thought I'd see one of them things. It's a man, sure enough, isn't it?"

"Men are not a half inch tall."

"How about pygmies?"

"Four feet. That's forty-eight inches, just ninety-six times as tall."

"Well—"

"What did you mean when you said you never thought you'd see one of them things? You don't seem one damn bit surprised."

"Oh, I'm a little bit surprised, Herb."

"Not enough."

"Maybe it's harder for a cop to show surprise, Herb. You get to expect anything."

"Not this."

"All right, Herb. Truth is, Abigail ain't the first. I never saw one before, but we been getting the reports. Frightened kids, housewives, old Ezra Bean who still farms his place up in Newtown, a frightened old lady in Bethel —she said her dog ate a mess of them—another lady over in Ridgefield, said her dog sniffed some out and they shot his nose full of little arrows, quarter of an inch long, had to take them out with tweezers. Of course, none of them really believed what they saw, and nobody else believed it either." He stared through the magnifying glass again. "Don't know that I believe it myself."

"Bows and arrows?"

"Little bugger has no clothes on. Kind of hard to believe."

"Bows and arrows mean intelligence," Herbert Cooke said worriedly.

"Ahh, who knows? Might have poked his nose into a bramble bush."

"Abigail's pretty upset. Says she killed a man."

"Baloney."

"Can I tell her she's clear, in a legal sense?"

"Of course. It was an accident anyway."

"What are you going to do with that?" Cooke asked, nodding at the flyswatter.

"Pick it off and put it in formaldehyde. You want the flyswatter back?"

"I don't think Abby would welcome it. You can't just leave him swimming in formaldehyde?"

"No, I don't suppose so. Maybe it's a case for the FBI, although I ain't heard nothing about this outside of Connecticut. Maybe I'll run over and see Judge Billings. He might have some ideas on the subject. You tell Abby not to worry."

"That's not easy," Herbert said. He himself was far from satisfied. Like several million other Americans, he had been brooding over the question of war and murder and Vietnam, and he had even thought seriously of switching his affiliation from the Congregational Church to the Quakers. It would be harder for Abigail, who came from many generations of Congregationalists, but they had discussed it, and he felt secure in his position as a man of conscience.

"Well, you tell her not to worry, and I'll have a talk with Judge Billings."

When Herbert Cooke returned to his home the following day, he was met by a wife whose face was set and whose eyes were bleak.

"I want to sell the house and move," she announced.

"Oh, come on, come on, Abby. You know you don't mean that. Not our house."

"Our house."

"You're upset again."

"Not again. Still. I didn't sleep all night. Today Billy got a splinter in his toe."

"It happens. The kids run around barefoot."

"I want to show you the splinter. I saved it." She led him to his desk, unfolded a piece of paper, and handed him the magnifying glass. "Look at it."

He peered through the glass at a tiny sliver of wood, less than a quarter of an inch long.

"Good heavens!"

"Yes."

"Incredible."

"Yes," his wife repeated.

"Barbed head—it could be metal. Looks like it."

"I don't care whether it's metal. I don't care what it looks like. I want to sell the house and get out of here."

"That's simply an emotional response," he assured her in his calmest and most legalistic tone of voice.

"I'm emotional."

"You're reacting to an unprecedented event. Outside of
Gulliver's Travels, this has never happened to anyone before, and if I am not mistaken, Gulliver's people were
three or four inches tall. A half inch is very disturbing."

"It's also very disturbing to live with the fact that
you've killed a man with a flyswatter."

A few days after this conversation, Abigail read an edi-
torial in the Danbury paper. In properly light and mock-
ing tones, it said: "Is it true, as the song puts it, that there
are fairies at the bottom of our gardens? A number of
otherwise sober citizens have been muttering that they
have seen very small people. How small? Anywhere from
half an inch to three-quarters of an inch, a diminution of
size that puts Gulliver to shame. We ourselves have not
encountered any of the little fellows, but we have an Irish
grandmother who reports numerous such encounters in
the Old Country. We might say that Irish Dew, taken in
sufficient quantities, will produce the same effect in any
locale."

Since the children were present, Abigail passed the
paper to her husband without comment. He read it, and
then he said:

"I asked Reverend Somers to stop by."

"Oh?"

"It's a moral question, isn't it? I thought it might put
your mind to rest."

Their daughter watched them curiously. There are no
secrets from children. "Why can't I play in the woods?"
Billy wanted to know.

"Because I say so," Abigail answered, a tack she had
never taken before.

"Effie Jones says there are little people in the woods,"
Billy continued. "Effie Jones says she squashed one of
them."

"Effie Jones is a liar, which everyone knows," his sister
said.

"I don't like to hear you call anyone a liar," Herbert said uncomfortably. "It's not very nice."

"We're such nice people," Abigail told herself. Yet she was relieved when Reverend Somers appeared later that evening. Somers was an eminently sensible man who looked upon the world without jaundice or disgust, not at all an easy task in the 1970s.

Somers tasted his sherry, praised it, and said that he was delighted to be with nice people, some of his nicest people.

"But like a doctor," Herbert said, "your hosts are never very happy."

"I don't know of any place in the Bible where happiness is specified as a normal condition of mankind."

"Last week I was happy," Abigail said.

"Let me plunge into some theology," Herbert said bluntly. "Do you believe that God made man in His own image?"

"Anthropomorphically—no. In a larger sense, yes. What is it, Herbert? The little people?"

"You know about them?"

"Know. Heard. It's all over the place, Herbert."

"Do you believe it?"

"I don't know what to believe."

"Believe it, Reverend. Abby swatted one. With the fly-swatter. Killed it. I brought it over to Chief Bradley."

"No."

"Yes," Abigail interjected bitterly.

"What was it?" the Reverend asked.

"I don't know," Herbert replied unhappily. "Under the magnifying glass, it was a man. A complete man about as big as a large ant. A white man."

"Why must you keep harping on the fact that it was a white man?" Abigail said.

"Well, it's just a matter of fact. It was a white man."

"You appear quite satisfied that it was a man."

"I thought it was a fly," Abigail interjected. "For

heaven's sake, the thing was not much bigger than a fly."

"Absolutely," Herbert agreed.

"What you both mean," Somers said slowly, "is that it looked like a man."

"Well—yes."

"Where is it now?"

"Chief Bradley put it into formaldehyde."

"I should like to have a look at it. We say it looks like a man. But what makes man? Is it not above all things the possession of a soul?"

"That's debatable," said Abby.

"Is it, my dear? We know man in two ways, as he is and as he is divinely revealed to us. Those two aspects add up to man. All else is of the animal and vegetable kingdom. We know man as a creature of our size. Divinely revealed, he is still a creature of our size."

"Not from outer space," Abby said.

"What does that mean?" her husband demanded.

"It means that from one of those wretched spaceships, the earth is the size of an orange, and that doesn't make man very big, does it?"

"For heaven's sake," Herbert said, "you are really blowing things out of proportion. You're talking about perspective, point of view. A man remains the same size no matter how far out into space you get."

"How do you know?" she asked with the reasonable unreasonableness of an intelligent woman.

"My dear, my dear," Somers said, "you are upset, we all are upset, and probably we shall be a good deal more upset before this matter is done with. But I do think you must keep a sense of proportion. Man is what God made him to be and what we know him to be. I am not an insensitive person. You know I have never wavered in my views of this wretched war in Vietnam—in spite of the difficulties in holding my congregation together. I speak to you, not as some Bible Belt fundamentalist, but as a person who believes in God in an indefinable sense."

"If He's indefinable, He's still rather large, isn't He? If He goes out into space a million light-years, how big are we to Him?"

"Abby, you're being contentious for no reason at all."

"Am I?" She unfolded a piece of paper and held it out to Somers with a magnifying glass. He peered at it through the glass and said words to the effect that the sliver of wood it contained looked like an arrow.

"It is an arrow. I took it out of Billy's toe. No, he didn't see what shot at him, but how long before he does? How long before he steps on one?"

"Surely there's some explanation for this—some new insect that appears remarkably manlike. Monkeys do, apes do, but one doesn't leap to the conclusion that they are men."

"Insects with blond hair and white skin and two arms and two legs who shoot arrows—really, Reverend Somers."

"Whatever it is, Abby, it is a part of the natural world, and we must accept it as such. If some of them are killed, well, that too is a part of our existence and their existence, not more or less than the natural calamities that overtake man—floods, earthquakes, the death of cities like ancient Pompeii."

"You mean that since they are very small, a flyswatter becomes a natural calamity."

"If you choose to put it that way—yes, yes, indeed."

Aside from a small squib in *The New York Times* about the strange behavior of some of the citizens of upper Fairfield County, the matter of the little people was not taken very seriously, and most of the local residents tended to dismiss the stories as the understandable result of a very hot summer. The Cookes did not sell their house, but Abigail Cooke gave up her habit of walking in the woods,

and even high grass gave her pause. She found that she
was looking at the ground more and more frequently and
sleeping less well. Herbert Cooke picked up a field mouse
that fairly bristled with the tiny arrows. He did not tell
his wife.

Judge Billings telephoned him. "Drop by about four,
Herb," he said. "A few people in my chambers. You'll be
interested."

Billings had already indicated to Herbert Cooke that
he considered him an excellent candidate for Congress
when the present incumbent—in his middle seventies—
stepped aside. It pleased Cooke that Billings called him
Herb, and he expected that the summons to his chambers
would have something to do with the coming elections.
Whereby he was rather surprised to find Chief Bradley
already there, as well as two other men, one of them a
Dobson of the FBI and the other a Professor Channing of
Yale, who was introduced as an entomologist.

"Herb here," the judge explained, "is the young fellow
whose wife swatted the thing—the first one we had. Now
we got a round dozen of them."

Channing took a flat wooden box out of his pocket—
about six inches square. He opened it and exhibited a
series of slides, upon each of which one of the tiny folk
was neatly pressed. Cooke glanced at it, felt his stomach
rise, and fought to control himself.

"In addition to which," the judge continued, "Herb has
a damn good head on his shoulders. He'll be our candidate
for the House one of these days and a damn important
man in the county. I thought he should be here."

"You must understand," said the FBI man, "that we've
already had our discussions on the highest level. The
Governor and a number of people from the state. Thank
God it's still a local matter, and that's what we're getting
at here."

"The point is," said Channing, "that this whole phenomenon is no more than a few years old. We have more or less mapped the beginning place of origin as somewhere in the woods near the Saugatuck Reservoir. Since then they've spread out six or seven miles in every direction. That may not seem like a lot, but if you accept their stride as a quarter inch compared to man's stride of three feet, you must multiply by one hundred and forty-four times. In our terms, they have already occupied a land area roughly circular and more than fifteen hundred miles in diameter. That's a dynamic force of terrifying implications."

"What the devil are they?" Bradley asked.

"A mutation—an evolutionary deviation, a freak of nature—who knows?"

"Are they men?" the judge asked.

"No, no, no, of course they're not men. Structurally, they appear to be very similar to men, but we've dissected them, and internally there are very important points of difference. Entirely different relationships of heart, liver, and lungs. They also have a sort of antenna structure over their ears, not unlike what insects have."

"Yet they're intelligent, aren't they?" Herbert Cooke asked. "The bows and arrows—"

"Precisely, and for that reason very dangerous."

"And doesn't the intelligence make them human?" the judge asked.

"Does it? The size and structure of a dolphin's brain indicate that it is as intelligent as we are, but does it make it human?"

Channing looked from face to face. He had a short beard and heavy spectacles, and a didactic manner of certainty that Herbert Cooke found reassuring.

"Why are they dangerous?" Cooke asked, suspecting that Channing was inviting the question.

"Because they came into being a year or two ago, no more, and they already have the bow and arrow. Our best educated guess is that they exist under a different subjective time sense than we do. We believe the same to hold true of insects. A day can be a lifetime for an insect, even a few hours, but to the insect it's his whole span of existence and possibly subjectively as long as our own lives. If that's the case with these creatures, there could be a hundred generations in the past few years. In that time, from their beginning to the bow and arrow. Another six months—guns. How long before something like the atomic bomb does away with the handicap of size? And take the question of population—you remember the checkerboard story. Put a grain of sand on the first box, two grains on the second, four grains on the third, eight grains on the fourth—when you come to the final box, there's not enough sand on all the beaches to satisfy it."

The discussion went on, and Herbert Cooke squirmed uneasily. His eyes constantly strayed to the slides on the table.

"Once it gets out . . ." the judge was saying.

"It can't get out," the FBI man said flatly. "They already decided that. When you think of what the kids and the hippies could do with this one—no, it's a question of time. When? That's up to you people."

"As soon as possible," Channing put in.

"What are you going to do?" Herbert asked.

"DDT's been outlawed, but this will be an exception. We've already experimented with a concentration of DDT—"

"Experimented?"

"We trapped about eighteen of them alive. The DDT is incredibly effective. With even a moderate concentration, they die within fifteen minutes."

"We'll have forty helicopters," the FBI man explained. "Spray from the air and do the whole thing between three and four A.M. People will be asleep, and most of them will never know it happened. Saturation spraying."

"It's rough on the bees and some of the animals, but we have no choice."

"Just consider the damn kids," Chief Bradley pointed out to Herbert. "Do you know they're having peace demonstrations in a place like New Milford? It's one thing to have the hippies out every half hour in New York and Washington and Los Angeles—but now we got it in our own backyard. Do you know what we'd have if the kids got wind that we're spraying these bugs?"

"How do they die?" Herbert asked. "I mean, when you spray them, how do they die?"

"The point is, Herb," Judge Billings put in, "that we need your image. There have been times when it's been a damn provoking image—I mean your wife riding around with that *Mother for Peace* sticker on her bumper and holding the vigils and all that kind of thing, not to mention that petition she's been circulating on this ecology business—it's just dynamite, this ecology thing—so I'll be frank to tell you it has been a mighty provoking image. But I suppose there's two sides to every coin, and I'm the first one to say that you can't wipe out a whole generation of kids; damn it, you can't even lock them up. You got to deal with them, and that's one of your virtues, Herb. You can deal with them. You have the image, and it's an honest image and it's worth its weight in gold to us. There'll be trouble, but we want to keep it at a low level. Those crazy Unitarians are already stirring up things, and I'm a Congregationalist myself, but I could name you two or three Congregationalist ministers who would stir up a hornest's nest if they were sitting here. There are others too, and I think you can deal with them."

"I was just wondering how they die when you spray them," Herbert said.

"That's just it," Channing said eagerly. "There may

not be much explaining to do. The DDT appears to
paralyze them almost instantly, even when it's not direct,
even when it's only a drift. They stop movement and then
they turn brown and wither. What's left is shapeless and
shriveled and absolutely beyond any identification. Have
a look at this slide."

He took one of the slides and held a magnifying glass
over it. The men crowded close to see, and Herbert found
himself joining them.

"It looks like last season's dead cockroach," said Bradley.

"We want you to set the time," Dobson, the FBI man,
told them. "It's your turf and your show."

"What about the dangers of the DDT?"

"Overrated—vastly overrated. We sure as hell don't rec-
ommend a return to it. The Department of Agriculture
has put its foot down on that, but the plain fact of the
matter is that we've been using DDT for years. One more
spray is not going to make a particle of difference. By the
time the sun rises, it's done with."

"The sooner the better," Chief Bradley said.

That night Herbert Cooke was awakened by the dron-
ing beat of the helicopters. He got up, went into the bathroom, and looked at his watch. It was just past three
o'clock in the morning. When he returned to bed, Abigail
was awake, and she asked him:

"What's that?"

"It sounds like a helicopter."

"It sounds like a hundred helicopters."

"Only because it's so still."

A few minutes later she whispered, "My God, why
doesn't it stop?"

Herbert closed his eyes and tried to sleep.

"Why doesn't it stop? Herb, why doesn't it stop?"

"It will. Why don't you try to sleep? It's some army
exercise. It's nothing to worry about."

"They sound like they're on top of us."

"Try to sleep, Abby."

Time passed, and presently the sound of the helicopters receded into the distance, faded, and then ceased. The silence was complete—enormous silence. Herbert Cooke lay in bed and listened to the silence.

"Herb?"

"I thought you were asleep."

"I can't sleep. I'm afraid."

"There's nothing to be afraid of."

"I was trying to remember how big the universe is."

"To what end, Abby?"

"Do you remember that book I read by Sir James Jean, the astronomer? I think he said the universe is two hundred million light-years from end to end—"

Herbert listened to the silence.

"How big are we, Herb?" she asked plaintively. "How big are we?"

4

The Hole in
the Floor

"You must have a lot of clout," Robinson said.

"I haven't any clout. My uncle has clout. He's a friend of the Commissioner."

"We never had anyone in the back seat before."

"Except a perpetrator," said Robinson, grinning. He was a black man with a round face and an infectious smile.

"If I had a brain in my head," McCabe said, "I would be a writer and not a cop. There's this guy out in the L.A. police force, and he's a writer. He wrote this book and it became a best seller, and he's loaded but he still wants to be a cop. Beats the hell out of me. I didn't read the book but I saw the movie. Did you see the movie?"

"I saw it."

"Good movie."

"It was a lousy movie," said Robinson.

"That's your opinion. L.A. isn't New York."

"You can say that again."

"You been to L.A.?" McCabe asked me. He was older

than Robinson, in his late thirties and going to fat, with a hard, flat face and small, suspicious blue eyes. I like the way he got along with Robinson; there was an easy give and take, and they never pushed each other.

McCabe took a call, and Robinson stepped on the gas and turned on his siren. "This is a mugging," McCabe said.

It was a purse snatch on 116th Street, involving two kids in their teens. The kids had gotten away, and the woman was shaken and tearful but unharmed. Robinson took down the descriptions of the kids and the contents of the purse, while McCabe calmed the woman and pushed the crowd on its way.

"There are maybe ten thousand kids in this city who will do a purse snatch or a mugging, and how do you catch them, and if you catch them, what do you do with them? You said you been to L.A.?"

"A few times, on and off."

"This is a sad city," Robinson said. "It's hanging on, but that's the most you can say. It's just hanging on."

"What's it like?" McCabe wanted to know.

"Downtown it's like this, maybe worse in some places."

"But in Hollywood, Beverly Hills, places like that?"

"It's sunny. When there's no smog."

"What the hell," said McCabe, "no overcoats, no snow— I got six more years, and then I think I'll take the wife and head west."

We stopped, and Robinson wrote out a ticket for a truck parked in front of a fire hydrant.

"You go through the motions," he said. "I guess that's the way it is. Everyone goes through the motions."

"You ever deliver a baby?" I asked him.

He grinned his slow, pleasant grin and looked at me in the rearview mirror.

"You ask McCabe."

"We did seven of them," McCabe said. "That's just since we been together. I ain't talking about rushing them to the hospital. I'm talking about the whole turn, and that includes slapping them across the ass to make them cry."

"One was twins," Robinson said.

"How did you feel? I mean when you did it, and there was the kid crying and alive?"

"You feel good."

"High as a kite," said Robinson. "It's a good feeling. You feel maybe the way a junkie feels when he can't make a connection and then finally he's got the needle in his arm. High."

"Does it make up for the other things?"

There was a long pause after that before McCabe asked me, "What other things?"

"One son of a bitch," Robinson said slowly, "he put his gun into my stomach and pulled the trigger three times. It don't make up for that."

"Gun misfired," McCabe explained. "Three times. A lousy little Saturday night special—happens maybe once in a thousand times."

"It don't make up for being black," Robinson said.

We cruised for the next ten minutes in silence. Possibly it was the last thing Robinson said; perhaps they resented having me in the back seat. Then they got a call, and McCabe explained that it was an accident in a house on 118th Street.

"It could be anything," Robinson said. "The floors collapse, the ceilings fall down, and the kids are eaten by rats. I grew up in a house like that. I held it against my father. I still hold it against him."

"Where can they go?"

"Away. Away is a big place."

"You can't just write about cops," McCabe said. "Cops are a reaction. A floor falls in and they call the cops. What the hell are we supposed to do? Rebuild these lousy rat-traps?"

We rolled into 118th Street, and there were half a dozen people standing in front of one of the tenements, and one of them told us that it was Mrs. Gonzales who put in the call and that her apartment was in the back, four flights up.

"What happened there?" McCabe wanted to know.

"Who knows? She don't let us in."

"Is she hurt?"

"She ain't hurt. She don't let us in."

We started up the stairs, McCabe and Robinson pushing their coats behind their guns, and myself allowing them to lead the way. A couple of the men outside started to follow us, but McCabe waved them back and told them to clear out. We climbed four flights of stairs, walked to the back of the narrow old-law tenement, and Robinson knocked on the door.

"Who is it?"

"Police," Robinson said.

She opened the door to the length of the safety chain, and Robinson and McCabe identified themselves. Then she let us in, through the kitchen, which is where the door is in most of the old-law tenements. The place was neat and clean. Mrs. Gonzales was a skinny little woman of about forty-five. Her husband, she told us, worked for Metropolitan Transit. Her son worked in a butcher shop on Lexington Avenue. She was all alone in the apartment, and she was on the verge of hysteria.

"It's all right now," McCabe said with surprising gentleness. "Just tell us what happened."

She shook her head.

"Something must have happened," Robinson said. "You called the police."

She nodded vigorously.

"All right, Mrs. Gonzales," Robinson said, "so something happened that shocked you. We know about that. It upsets you, it makes you sick. You feel cold and feel like maybe you want to throw up. Do you feel cold now?"

She nodded.

Robinson took a sweater off a hook in the kitchen. "Put this on. You'll feel better."

She put on the sweater.

"Anyone in there?" McCabe asked, nodding toward the other rooms.

"No," she whispered.

"Got any brandy—whiskey?"

She nodded toward a cupboard, and I went there and found a bottle of rum. I poured a few ounces into a glass and handed it to her. She drank it, made a face, and sighed.

"Now tell us what happened."

She nodded and led the way out of the kitchen, through a room which served as a dining room-living room, clean, rug on the floor, cheap ornate furniture, polished and loved, to the door of the next room, which had two beds that served as couches, a chest of drawers, and a hole in the middle of the floor about three and a half or four feet across.

"Goddamn floor fell in," said McCabe.

"The way they build these places," said Robinson.

"The way they built them seventy-five years ago," I said.

Mrs. Gonzales said nothing, stopped at the door to the room, and would go no farther.

"Who lives underneath?" McCabe asked.

"Montez. He is a teacher. No one is home now—except the devil."

Robinson entered the bedroom and walked gingerly toward the hole. The ancient floor creaked under his feet but held. He stopped a foot short of the edge of the hole and looked down. He didn't say anything, just stood there and looked down.

"The building should be condemned," said McCabe, "but then where do they go? You want to write about problems, here's a problem. The whole goddamn city is a problem."

Still Robinson stared silently into the hole. I envisioned a corpse below or the results of some unspeakable murder. I started into the room.

"Take it easy," McCabe warned me. "The floor's rotten. We don't want you down there. What do you think?" he asked Robinson.

Still no answer from Robinson.

I moved carefully in on one side of the room, McCabe following on the other side. We both reached the hole at the same time. Robinson was in front of the hole, his back to the door. McCabe and I stood on either side of him.

Even before my eyes registered what was down there, I was conscious of the smell. It reminded me of the odor of jasmine, yet it was different. It was something I had never known before, as indescribable as it was different, and it came on a slow current of warm air that I can only think of as silver. It's not possible to explain why a breath of air should evoke the image of silver, but there it was.

And then I saw what I saw. I saw what McCabe saw and what Robinson saw, so I did not dream it and I did not imagine it. About ten feet beneath the hole was a grassy sward. Its appearance suggested that it had been mowed, the way an old English lawn is mowed, yet something about it argued that the thick, heavy turf grew that way and had never known a mower's blade. Nor was the grass green the way we know green; it appeared to be overlaid with a glow of lilac.

No one of us spoke. No one suggested that this might be the floor of Mr. Montez's apartment and that the teacher specialized in horticulture; we knew it was not the floor of Mr. Montez's apartment, and that was all we knew. The only sound in the apartment was the gentle sobbing of Mrs. Gonzales.

Then Robinson crouched down, sprawled his huge bulk back from the edge of the hole, and let his head and shoulders hang over, bracing himself with his hands. The rotten floor creaked under him.

"Watch it!" McCabe exclaimed. "You'll be down there on your head."

He was wonderful. He was what only an old New York City cop could be, possessed of a mentality in which there was neither the unexpected nor the impossible. Anything could happen in New York, and it usually did.

"What do you see?" I asked Robinson.

"More of it. Just more of it." He drew himself back and stood up, and he looked from my face to McCabe's face.

"We're four stories high," McCabe said bleakly, his universe finally tilting on edge.

"A lot more of it," said Robinson.

"I'll phone it in. I'll tell them there's a cow pasture on the fourth floor of an old-law tenement."

"It's no cow pasture," Robinson said.

"Then what the hell is it? A mirage?"

"I'm going down there," Robinson said.

"Like hell you are!"

Robinson's round face was no longer jovial, no longer the easy, controlled face of a black cop in New York, who knows how much to push and just when to push. He looked at McCabe, smiling a thin, humorless smile, and he asked him what he thought was down there through the hole to teacher Montez's apartment.

"How the hell should I know?"

"I know."

"My ass, you know!"

"What's down there?" I asked Robinson, my voice shaking. "What did you see?"

"The other side of the coin."

"What the hell does that mean?" McCabe demanded.

"Man," Robinson sighed, "you been white just too god-damn long."

"I'm going to call in," McCabe said. "You hear me, Robinson? I'm going to call in, and then I'm going to get the keys from the super—if there is one in this lousy rat-trap—and I'm going to go into Montez's apartment and I'm going to look right up your ass through that hole, and we'll see who grows grass four stories up. And until I do, you don't go down there. You understand?"

"Sure, man. I understand," Robinson answered softly.

Then McCabe pushed past the sobbing Mrs. Gonzales and slammed the kitchen door behind him. As if his slamming the door had created a current, the perfumed air rose out of the hole and filled the bedroom.

"What did you see down there?" I asked Robinson.

"Have a look?" Robinson suggested.

I shook my head. Nothing on earth would persuade me to lie belly down on that creaking floor and hang over the edge the way Robinson had before. Robinson was watching me.

"Afraid?"

I nodded.

"You know what's going to happen when McCabe gets the super and they go into that apartment under us? Just like he said—he'll be standing there looking right up my asshole—then it'll be some kind of optical illusion, and two or three weeks—man, in two, three weeks we won't even remember we saw it."

"It's an illusion," I agreed.

"Smell it!"

"Jesus Christ, you're looking at something that isn't there!"

"But you and me, mister, and that lady over there"—he

waved one arm in a circle—"that's real. That's no illusion."

"That's real," I said.

He stared at me a long moment, shook his head, then sat down on the edge of the break in the floor, slid down, rolled over, hanging on by his hands, and then dropped, landing in a crouch on the turf. He brought himself erect and turned in a three-hundred-and-sixty-degree circle, his eyes sweeping over what he saw. Like the grass he stood upon, he was bathed in a kind of violet sunshine.

"Robinson!"

He didn't hear me. It was obvious that he didn't hear. He raised his face to where I should have been, his dark skin bathed in the lilac sunshine, and whatever his eyes saw, they did not see me. The strange light turned his dark brown skin into a kind of smoky gold. He looked around again, grinning with delight.

"Hey, man!" he called out. "Hey, man—you still up there?"

"I'm here. Can you hear me?"

"Man, if you're still there, I can't hear you, I can't see you, and you better believe me, it don't bother me one bit!"

Mrs. Gonzales screamed. She screamed two or three times and then settled for sobbing.

"Tell McCabe," yelled Robinson, "tell McCabe to take his prowl car and shove it up his goddamn ass! Tell Mc-Cabe—"

I never knew what else he would have told McCabe to do, because at that moment McCabe kicked in the door of Montez's apartment, and then there were the two of them, McCabe and Robinson, standing in a litter of broken laths and chunks of plaster, just the two of them, standing in the litter and staring at each other.

McCabe looked up at me and said, "Stay back from the edge, because the whole lousy ceiling's coming down. I called emergency. We're going to empty the building, so tell that Gonzales woman to put on her coat and come downstairs." Then he turned to Robinson. "You had to do it. You couldn't stay up there. You had to show you're an athlete."

To which Robinson said nothing at all.

Back in the prowl car, later, I asked Robinson what he had seen.

"In Montez's apartment? The man has a lot of books. You know, sometimes I say to myself I should have been a teacher instead of a cop. My brother-in-law's a teacher. A principal. He makes more money than I do and he's got some respect. A cop has no respect. You break your back and risk your life, and they spit in your face."

"You can say that again," McCabe said.

"We once pulled four people out of a burning building on One hundred fortieth Street—my own people—and some son of a bitch clipped me with a brick. For what? For saving four people?"

"You know what I mean. When you stood there on the grass and looked around you, what did you see?"

"A lousy old-law tenement that should have been torn down fifty years ago," said Robinson.

"You take a car like this," said McCabe, "it's unusual to you. You pull a few strings downtown, and they say, OK, sit in the car and write a story about it. For us it's a grind, day in, day out, one lousy grind." He took a call on the car radio. "Liquor store this time. West One hundred seventeenth, Brady's place. You know," he said to me, "they rip off that place every month, regular as clockwork."

The siren going, we tore up Amsterdam Avenue to 117th Street.

5
General Hardy's Profession

Miss Kanter was not quite certain whether she was in love with Dr. Blausman or not, but she felt that the privilege of working for such a man repaid and balanced her devotion, even though Dr. Blausman never made a pass at her or even allowed her that peculiar intimacy that many men have with their secretaries. It was not that Dr. Blausman was cold; he was happily married and utterly devoted to his work and his family, and brilliant. Miss Kanter had wept very real tears of joy when he was elected president of the Society.

In her own right, Miss Kanter was skilled and devoted, and after five years with Dr. Blausman she had developed a very keen clinical perception of her own. When she took a history of a new patient, it was not only complete but pointed and revealing. In the case of Alan Smith, however, there was a noticeable hiatus.

"Which troubles me somewhat," Dr. Blausman remarked. "I dislike taking anyone who isn't a referral."

"He has been referred, or recommended, I suppose. He mentioned the air shuttle, which makes me think he is either from Washington or Boston. Washington, I would say. I imagine that it would make trouble for him if it got out that he was going into therapy."

"Trouble?"

"You know how the government is about those things."

"You must have found him very appealing."

"Very good-looking, Doctor. You know, I am a woman." Miss Kanter seized opportunities to remind Dr. Blausman. "But very desperate for help. If he is government and high government—well, that might be very meaningful, might it not?"

"Still, he refuses to say who recommended him?"

"Yes. But I'm sure you'll get it out of him."

"You told him my fee?"

"Of course."

"Was his face familiar?"

"It was one of those faces that seem to be. But I have no idea who he really is."

Neither did Dr. Blausman have any sure idea of who the new patient was. It was the following day, and across the desk from Dr. Blausman sat a strongly built, handsome man, with pale blue eyes, iron-gray hair, and a square jaw that would have done credit to a Western star of the thirties. He was about forty-five years old, six feet or so in height, and appeared to be in excellent physical condition. He was nervous, but that was a symptom that brought patients into the office in the first place.

"Well, Mr. Smith," Dr. Blausman began, "suppose you tell me something about yourself, what made you seek me out, who referred you to me, your problems—"

"I have only the most rudimentary knowledge of psycho-analysis, Doctor."

"That doesn't matter. It's important that my knowledge

should be a little more than rudimentary. Which I hope it is. But for the moment, forget about psychoanalysis. I am a psychiatrist, and I prefer to think of my work as psychotherapy. Does the thought of psychoanalysis disturb you?"

"I suppose it does. The couch and all that—"

"You can lie down if you wish, or you can sit in a chair. That's not important, Mr. Smith. The point is to get at the root of what troubles you and to see whether we can alleviate the pain. We do that by establishing a relationship. So, you see, you have to be rather forthright. It is true that in the course of therapy, even lies can be revealing, but that's not a good way to begin."

"I don't understand you."

"I think you do. I must know who you are. Otherwise—"

"I told you that my name is Alan Smith."

"But it isn't," Blausman said gently.

"How do you know?"

"If I were not adept enough at my discipline to know, you would be making a mistake in coming to me."

"I see." The patient sat in silence for a moment or two. "And if I refuse to give you any other name?"

"Then I am afraid you must seek help elsewhere. There is a sufficient unknown in a person who meets me forthrightly. In one who doesn't—well, it is impossible."

The patient nodded and appeared to reflect on the doctor's words. "How confidential is your treatment?"

"Totally."

"Do you make tapes?"

"No."

"Do you take notes?"

"In most cases, yes. If there were sufficient reason not to keep notes, I would forgo it." When the patient still hesitated, Dr. Blausman said, "Perhaps you would prefer to think about it and return tomorrow?"

"No, that won't be necessary. I also pride myself on

being a judge of character, and I think I can trust you. My name is Franklin Hardy. General Franklin Hardy. I am a three-star general, second in command at the War Board. A three-star general who is second in command at the War Board does not consult a psychoanalyst."

"Have you thought of resigning or taking a leave of absence, General Hardy?"

"I have thought of it—yes. My pride will not allow me to resign, and the situation today is too grave for me to take a leave of absence. Also, I don't think I am unable to perform my duties. My country has a large investment in me, Dr. Blausman. I don't feel it is my right to play fast and loose with that."

"And how did you come to me? You are stationed in Washington, are you not?"

"At the Pentagon."

"So if we were to have three sessions a week—and I am afraid that would be minimal—you would have to do a good deal of commuting. Isn't that a burden?"

"I want this kept secret, and that might be impossible with a local man."

"But why me?"

"I read a paper of yours and I was very impressed by it. Your monograph on the Amnesia Syndrome."

"Oh? But surely you don't feel you have amnesia?"

"Perhaps—I don't know."

"Very interesting." Dr. Blausman stared at the General thoughtfully. "Since you read my paper, you are aware that there is an enormous variety of amnesia, loss of identity being most common in the public mind. You obviously do not suffer that. There are childhood amnesias, adolescent amnesias, traumatic amnesias, and a hundred other varieties, due to shock, brain injury, drugs, senility—well, I could go on and on. Why do you feel you suffer from amnesia?"

The General considered this for a while, and then he spoke flatly and abruptly. "I am not sure I know who I am."

Dr. Blausman smiled slightly. "Most interesting indeed. But in what sense? I have many young patients who feel a desperate need to know who they are. But that is in a religious, philosophical, or teleological sense. What meaning has their presence on earth?"

"Not exactly."

"You told me that you are General Franklin Hardy. I could ask you to show me your papers, but that's hardly necessary."

"Not at all." The general went into his pocket and revealed a series of identity cards. He smiled a very engaging smile. "Of course, they are not my only source of information. I have been with the army for twenty-seven years, and there are no gaps in my memory. I have served in World War Two, in Korea, and in Vietnam. As you may recall."

Dr. Blausman nodded. "I read the papers." He waited a long moment. "Go on, sir."

"All right, let me be specific. Three nights ago, I awakened. I am not married, Doctor. As I said, I awakened about four o'clock in the morning, and I was not General Hardy."

"You are sure you were awake?"

"Absolutely sure. I was not dreaming. I got out of bed, and I was someone else."

"In a strange place? I mean, was your bedroom strange to you? Was it completely dark?"

"No, I could see. I don't draw the blinds, and there was moonlight. Was it strange to me?" He frowned and closed his eyes. "No—not entirely. I appeared to have a vague memory of a room that should have been completely familiar. I wondered what I was doing there. I felt that I should know."

"And then?"

"And then I was myself again, and it was over. But I couldn't get back to sleep. I was terribly shaken. I am not a man with poor nerves. I cannot remember being so shaken before."

Dr. Blausman glanced at his watch. "I'm afraid our time is over for today. Can you come back on Wednesday, the same time?"

"Then you will—?"

"Help you? Treat you? Yes, however you wish to see it."

When the doctor took his break for lunch, he said to his secretary, "You can make up a new history for Mr. Smith, Miss Kanter. He'll be back on Wednesday."

"Did you crack the mystery?"

"If you think of it that way. He's General Franklin Hardy."

"What!"

"Yes, General Hardy."

"And—and you—hell, it's none of my business."

"Exactly. I am not a moralist or a jurist, Miss Kanter. I am a physician."

"But, my God, Vietnam is not just a war. You know his record."

"What would you say if he came here bleeding, Miss Kanter? Would it be proper to put a tourniquet on him? Or would it be more moralistic to allow him to bleed to death?"

"Are you asking me, Doctor?"

"No, I am telling you, Miss Kanter."

"You don't have to get angry. Mine is a normal, human reaction. Anyway, it is a comfort to know that he has flipped out."

"He has not, as you put it, flipped out. Furthermore, this is to be absolutely confidential. He asked for my confidence, and I gave it to him. No one is to know that he is a patient of mine, not your father, not your mother, not your boyfriend—no one. Do you understand?"

"Loud and clear." Miss Kanter sighed.

Sitting opposite Dr. Blausman in a comfortable chair, his legs stretched out, General Hardy remarked that he had not thought of therapy in just this manner.

"It's the end product that counts, General—to find out why. Do you dream a great deal?"

"As much as the next one, I suppose. I don't remember them."

"I'd like you to takes notes. Keep a pencil and pad next to your bed. Now the night this happened—it was not the first time?"

"No, not the first time."

"When was the first time?"

"Two years ago, in Vietnam. We had been set back on our heels by Charlie's big offensive, and we had taken some pretty heavy losses. There was a lot of loose talk, and at one of our meetings the use of tactical atomic weapons was put on the agenda. Against my will, mind you. No sane or reasonable man can even think of tactical atomic weapons without going into a cold sweat, but since they were determined to talk about them, I decided to let them talk and get it out of their systems. After all, they could do nothing without my vote. I listened to the discussion, and there was one idiot there—who shall be nameless—who was all for using the tacticals and ending the war in hours. Of course it wouldn't have ended the war—no way—but he was off on a laboratory kick, that we'd never know how they worked until we worked them, and this was the one place it made sense to experiment. I kept my mouth shut, because there is nothing to defeat an argument like its own loopholes, and then it happened."

"What happened?"

"I was no longer General Hardy. I was someone else, and I was listening to this featherbrain and laughing inside at his whole proposition."

"Laughing? In what way?"

"Not contempt, not disapproval—I was laughing the way you laugh at a kid who has a new toy and has gone hog-wild with it. I was amused and—" He broke off.

"What were you going to say?"

The General remained silent.

"I am not a Congressional Committee," Blausman said softly. "I am not the public. I am a physician. I am not here to confront you or expose you, but to help you. If you don't want that help—well, the door is open."

"I know the damn door is open!" the General cried. "Do you think I'd be here if I could live with this? I was going to say that I was amused and delighted."

"Why didn't you say it?"

"Because the *I* is a lie. Not me. Not Franklin Hardy. The other one."

"Why do you say the other one?" Blausman asked. "Why not the other man?"

"I don't know."

"You have read about possession? By evil entities?"

"Yes."

"It has interesting psychological references. Do you have the feeling—I only speak of the feeling—that you were possessed?"

"No!"

"You appear very certain."

"I am certain," the General said emphatically.

"Why?"

"Because this is myself. Because the syndrome—as you call it—is not being possessed or used or manipulated, but simply remembering. I remember who I am."

"Who?"

"That's the damn trick. It passes too quickly."

"At this meeting, how long did this memory last?"

"A minute. A little more, a little less."

"And as I understand it," Dr. Blausman said carefully, "during that time you were delighted and amused at the thought of using atomic tactical weapons. Will you accept that?"

"You're asking me do I have the guts to?" the General said harshly. "All right, I do. I accept your statement, but not as Franklin Hardy. I accept it as the man who was amused."

"Whom you insist is yourself?"

"Yes. Do you understand now why I commute from Washington each day to see a psychiatrist?"

"What was the outcome of the meeting?"

"You know that. Atomic weapons are not firecrackers. We squashed the whole notion."

On his next visit, Dr. Blausman returned to the night-time incident, asking the General whether he had been awakened from sleep at other times.

"Yes."

"How many times?"

Hardy thought for a while. "Fourteen—or thirteen."

"Always the same time?"

"No. Sometimes earlier, sometimes later."

"Does one occasion stand out more than any other?"

"Yes." Then the General clamped his square jaw shut, and his pale blue eyes avoided the doctor's. The doctor waited.

"But you don't want to talk about it," Blausman said at last. "Why?"

"God damn you to hell, must you know everything?"

"Not everything. I don't ask you who you are sleeping with, or for the secret plans of the War Board, or what your golf score is," Blausman said gently. "If you had a piece of shrapnel in your left arm, I would not be fussing over your right foot. By the way, were you ever wounded?"

"No."

"Amazing luck, with your experience. Now let's go back to this waking up at night. That one occasion you don't want to talk about. It is nothing you are afraid of."

"How do you know?"

"You get disturbed but not frightened. There's a difference. What happened that night, General?"

"I woke up, and I was someone else."

"You were someone else. What makes that night stand out?"

"You won't let go, will you?"

"Otherwise I am taking your money under false pretenses," Blausman said gently. "So you might as well tell me about that night."

"All right. I woke up. It was last May, and I was still in Vietnam. It was almost dawn. I was myself—not Hardy— and God almighty, I felt good. I felt like I had swallowed ten grains of Dexedrine and put down a pint of bourbon without getting drunk. Christ, what power, what sheer physical strength and joy! I wanted to run, to leap, to use my strength, as if I had been in a straitjacket for years. I felt that I was complete."

"For how long?"

"Two or three minutes."

"You went outside?"

"How did you know?" the General asked curiously. "Yes, I went outside in my robe. It was like walking on air, the sun just coming up, the kind of clean, cool, wonderful morning you get sometimes in that part of Vietnam. There was an iron fence in front of my quarters. Pointed bars, like a row of spears, an inch thick. I reached out and bent one of them, like I might bend rubber."

"You're a strong man."

"Not that strong. Well—then it was gone. I was Franklin Hardy again."

"Why hesitate to tell me?" Blausman asked.

"I don't know."

"Do you remember what you said a moment ago? You said that when you woke up, you were yourself, not General Hardy. That's rather odd, isn't it?"

"Did I say that?"

"Yes."

"It is odd," Hardy admitted, frowning. "I always said I was someone else, didn't I?"

"Until now."

"What do you make of it?"

"What do you make of it, General? That's the important thing."

When the General had left, Dr. Blausman asked Miss Kanter whether Alexander the Great had ever been wounded.

"I was a history dropout. They let me substitute sociology. Does the General think he's Alexander the Great?"

"How about Napoleon?"

"Was he wounded? Or does the General think he's Napoleon?"

"I want you to hire a researcher," Dr. Blausman said. "Let him pick up the three hundred most important military leaders in history. I want to know how many died in battle and how many were wounded."

"Are you serious?"

"Deadly so."

"As long as you pay for it," Miss Kanter said.

In the next session, Dr. Blausman asked the General about dreams. "You have been taking notes?"

"Once."

"Only once?"

"It appears that I dreamed only once. Or remembered only once long enough to get the notebook."

"Tell me about it."

"As much as I can remember. I was driving a truck."

"What kind of a truck? I want you to be very specific and to try to remember every detail you can."

"It was a tank truck. I know that. It was a shiny metal tank truck, strong motor, six speeds forward—" He closed his eyes and then shook his head.

"All right, it was a tank truck. Oil—milk—chemicals—chocolate syrup—which one? Try to think, try to visualize it."

The General kept his eyes closed. His handsome face was set and intent, his brow furrowed. "It was a tank truck, all right, a big, gutsy son of a bitch. The gearing was marked on the shift bar, but I knew it. I didn't have to be coached. I got out of it once, walked around it. Pipes—"

"What kind of pipes?"

"Black plastic, I guess. Beautiful pumping equipment. I remember thinking that whoever built that job knew what he was doing."

"Why did you get out of it?"

"I thought I had to use it."

"For what?" Blausman insisted. "For what?"

He shook his head, opened his eyes now. "I don't know."

"Fire truck?"

"No—never."

"Then you got back in the truck?"

"Yes. I started off again. In low gear, she whined like some kind of mad cat."

"Where were you? What was the place like?"

"A dead place. Like desert, only it wasn't desert. It was a place that had once been alive, and now it was dead and withered."

"Withered? Do you mean there were trees? Plants?"

The General shook his head. "It was desert. Nothing grew there."

"You started the truck again. Where were you going?"

"I don't know."

"Think about it. What were you?"

"What do you mean, what was I?"

"What was your profession?"

"I told you I was driving a truck."

"But was that your profession?" Blausman pressed him. "Did you think of yourself as a truck driver?"

After a moment of thought, the General said, "No. I didn't think of myself as a truck driver."

"Then what?"

"I don't know. I just don't know. What damn difference does it make?"

"All the damn difference in the world." Blausman nodded. "A man is what he does. Did you ever notice the way kids talk about what they are going to be when they grow up? They will be what they do. A man is his profession, his work. What was the profession of the man who was driving the truck?"

"I told you I don't know."

"You were driving the truck. Who were you? Were you General Hardy?"

"No."

"How were you dressed? Did you wear a uniform?"

Again General Hardy closed his eyes.

"Did you bring your notes with you?" the doctor asked.

"I know what was in my notes."

"Then you wore a uniform?"

"Yes," Hardy whispered.

"What kind?"

Hardy frowned and clenched his fists.

"What kind of a uniform?" Blausman persisted.

Hardy shook his head.

"Try to remember," Blausman said gently. "It's important."

Blausman took him to the door, and as it closed behind him, Miss Kanter said, "God, he's handsome."

"Yes, isn't he?"

"I wonder what it's like to be a General's wife?"

"You're losing your moral principles, Miss Kanter."

"I am simply speculating, which has nothing to do with morality."

"What about the research?"

"My goodness," said Miss Kanter, "you only told me about it the day before yesterday."

"Then this is the third day. What have you got?"

"I gave it to Evelyn Bender, who is a friend of mine and teaches history at Hunter College, and she was absolutely enthralled with the idea and she's going to charge you a hundred and fifty dollars."

"I said, what have you got?"

"Now?"

"Right now. Call her up."

Miss Kanter started to argue, looked at Dr. Blausman, and then called Evelyn Bender at Hunter College. Blausman went back to his office and his next patient. When that patient had left, Miss Kanter informed Dr. Blausman, rather tartly, that Mrs. Bender had only begun the project.

"She must have some indications. Did you ask her that?"

"Knowing you, I asked her. She's a scholar, you know, and they hate to guess."

"But she guessed."

"She thinks that perhaps ninety percent died in bed. She indicated that very few wounds are recorded."

"Keep after her."

There was a noticeable difference about General Hardy when he came back for his next visit. He sat down in the comfortable armchair that substituted for the couch, and he stared at Dr. Blausman long and thoughtfully before he said anything at all. His blue eyes were very cold and very distant.

"You've been thinking about your profession," Blausman said.

"Whose profession? This time you say my profession."

"I was interested in what your reaction would be."

"I see. Do you know how I spent the weekend?"

"Tell me."

"Reading up on schizophrenia."

"Why did you do that?" the doctor asked.

"Curiosity—reasonable curiosity. I wondered why you had never mentioned it."

"Because you are not schizophrenic."

"How do you know?"

"I have been in practice twenty-three years, General Hardy. It would be rather odd if I could not spot schizophrenia."

"In anyone?"

"Yes, in anyone. Certainly after the second visit."

"Then if I am not schizophrenic, Dr. Blausman, what explanation do you have for my condition?"

"What explanation do you have, General?"

"Well, now—the neurotic finds his own source, uncovers his own well of horror—is that it, Doctor?"

"More or less."

"Dreams are very important in the Freudian scheme of things. Are you a Freudian analyst, Doctor?"

"Every analyst is more or less a Freudian, General. He developed the techniques of our discipline. We have perhaps changed many of his techniques, modified many of his premises, but we remain Freudians, even those of us who angrily repudiate the label."

"I was speaking of dreams."

"Of course," Blausman agreed calmly. "Dreams are important. The patient uses them to deal with his problems.

But instead of the realities of his waking world, he clothes his problem in symbols. Sometimes the symbols are very obscure, very obscure indeed. Sometimes they are not. Sometimes they are obvious."

"As in my dream?"

"Yes, as in your dream."

"Then if you understood the symbols, why not tell me?"

"Because that would accomplish nothing of consequence. It is up to you to discover the meaning of the symbols. And now you know."

"You're sure of that?"

"I think so, yes."

"And the truck?"

"An exterminator's truck, obviously. I see you have remembered who you are."

"I am General Franklin Hardy."

"That would make you schizophrenic. I told you before that you are not schizophrenic."

"You say you have been in practice twenty-three years. Have you ever had a case like mine before, Doctor?"

"In a non-schizophrenic? No."

"Then does it make medical history of sorts?"

"Perhaps. I would have to know more about it."

"I admire your scientific detachment."

"Not so scientific that I am without very ordinary curiosity. Who are you, sir?"

"Before I answer that, let me pose a question, Doctor. Has it never occurred to you that in the history and practice of what we call mankind, there is a certain lack of logic?"

"It has occurred to me."

"What do you make of it?"

"I am a psychiatrist, General. I deal with psychosis and neurosis, neither of which is logical. Understandable, yes. Logical, no."

"You miss the point."

"Do I?" Blausman said patiently. "Then what is the point?"

"The point is fantastic."

"There is very little that astonishes me."

"Good. Then allow me to put it to you this way. The earth is a beautiful, rich, and splendid planet. It has all things that man desires, but none of these things is limitless, not the air, not the water, not even the fertility of the land. Let us postulate another planet very similar to earth— but used up, Doctor, used up. There are men on this planet as there are men here, but somewhat more advanced technologically. Like many men, they are selfish and selfseeking, and they want the earth. But they want the earth without its human population. They need the earth for their own purposes. I see you doubt me."

"The notion is certainly ingenious."

"And from that you conclude that madmen are ingenious. Let me go on with my premise, and since you have assured me that I am not schizophrenic, you can ponder over the precise quality of my madness."

"By all means," Blausman agreed.

"They could attack the earth, but that would mean grave losses and even the possibility of defeat—no matter how small that possibility is. So some time ago, they hit upon another plan. They would train men for a particular profession, train them very well indeed, and then they would bring these men to earth, put them into positions of great power, and then induce a conditioned amnesia. Thus, these men would know what they had to do, what they were trained to do, yet be without the knowledge of why they do what they must do."

"Absolutely fascinating," Blausman said. "And in your case, the amnesia broke."

"I think it is a limited thing in every case. A time comes

when we remember, but more clearly than I remembered. We know our profession, and in time we remember why we have been trained to this profession."

"And your profession?" Blausman asked.

"Of course, we are exterminators. I thought you understood that from the dream. So, Doctor, you would say I am cured, would you not?"

"Ah—there you have me." Blausman smiled.

"You don't believe me? You really don't believe me?"

"I don't know. What are your intentions, General? Are you going to kill me?"

"Why on earth should I kill you?"

"You defined your profession."

"One small, overweight New York psychiatrist? Come, come, Dr. Blausman—you have your own delusions of grandeur. I am an exterminator, not a murderer."

"But since you have told me what you are—"

Now it was the General's turn to smile. "My dear Dr. Blausman, what will you do? Will you take my story to the mayor, the governor, the President—the FBI, the press? How long would you maintain your professional status? Would you tell a story about little green men, about flying saucers? No, there is no need to kill you, Doctor. How inconvenient, how embarrassing that would be!" He rose to leave.

"This does not negate your bill," Blausman said. He could think of nothing else to say.

"Of course not. Send it to me in Washington."

"And just for my own parting shot, I don't believe one damn word you've said."

"Precisely, Doctor."

The General left and the doctor pulled himself together before he strode into the outer office and snapped at Miss Kanter: "Get his history and put it in the files. He won't come back."

"Really? Evelyn Bender just called and said she can have the survey by Wednesday."

"Tell her to tear it up, and send her a check. Cancel the rest of my appointments today. I'm going home."

"Is anything wrong?"

"No, Miss Kanter—not one damn thing. Everything is precisely the way it has always been."

6
Show Cause

Understandably, it was couched in modern terms; in the United States, on the three great networks in radio and in television, in England on BBC, and in each country according to its most effective wavelength. The millions and millions of people who went burrowing into their Bibles found a reasonable facsimile in Exodus 32, 9 and 10: "And the Lord said unto Moses, I have seen this people, and behold, it is a stiff-necked people: now therefore let me alone, that my wrath may wax hot against them, and that I may consume them."

The radio and television pronouncement said simply, "You must show cause why the people of Earth shall not be destroyed." And the signature was equally simple and direct: "I am the Lord your God."

The announcement was made once a day, at eleven A.M. in New York City, ten o'clock in Chicago, seven in Honolulu, two in the morning in Tokyo, midnight in Bangkok, and so forth around the globe. The voice was deep, resonant, and in the language of whatever people listened to it, and the signal was of such intensity that it preempted whatever program happened to be on the air at the moment.

The first reaction was inevitable and predictable. The Russians lashed out at the United States, holding that since the United States, by their lights, had committed every sin in the book in the name of God, they would hardly stop short at fouling up radio and television transmission. The United States blamed the Chinese, and the Chinese blamed the Vatican. The Arabs blamed the Jews, and the French blamed Billy Graham, and the English blamed the Russians, and the Vatican held its peace and began a series of discreet inquiries.

The first two weeks of the daily pronouncement were almost entirely devoted to accusation. Every group, body, organization, sect, nation that had access to power was accused, while the radio engineers labored to find the source of the signal. The accusations gradually perished in the worldwide newspaper, television, and radio debate on the subject, and the source of the signal was not found. The public discussions during those first two weeks are a matter of public record; the private ones are not, which makes the following excerpts of some historical interest:

THE KREMLIN

REZNOV: "I am not a radio engineer. Comrade Grinowski is a radio engineer. If I were Comrade Grinowski, I would go back to school for ten years. It is preferable to ten years in Siberia."

GRINOWSKI: "Comrade Reznov speaks, I am sure, as an expert radio engineer."

BOLOV: "Insolence, Comrade Grinowski, is no substitute for competence. Comrade Reznov is a Marxist, which allows him to penetrate to the heart of the matter."

GRINOWSKI: "You are also a Marxist, Comrade Bolov, and you are also Commissar of Communications. Why haven't you penetrated to the heart of the matter?"

REZNOV: "Enough of this bickering. You have every resource of Soviet science at your disposal, Comrade Grinowski. This is not merely a matter of jamming our signals; it is an attack upon our basic philosophy."

GRINOWSKI: "We have used every resource of Soviet science."

REZNOV: "And what have you come up with?"

GRINOWSKI: "Nothing. We don't know where the signals originate."

REZNOV: "Then what do you suggest, Comrade Bolov—in the light of Comrade Grinowski's statement?"

BOLOV: "You can shoot Comrade Grinowski or you can invite in the Metropolitan or both. The Metropolitan is waiting outside."

REZNOV: "Who asked the Metropolitan here?"

GRINOWSKI: (*with a small smile*) "I did."

THE WHITE HOUSE

THE PRESIDENT: "Where's Billy? I told him we start at two o'clock. Where is he?"

THE SECRETARY OF STATE: "I called him myself. We might hear from Professor Foster of MIT meanwhile."

THE PRESIDENT: "I want Billy to hear what Professor Foster has to say."

PROFESSOR FOSTER: "I have a very short statement. I have several copies. I can give a copy to Billy or I can read it again."

THE ATTORNEY GENERAL: "I say CBS is at the bottom of the whole matter. CIA agrees with me."

THE FEDERAL COMMUNICATIONS COMMISSIONER: "CBS is not at the bottom of it. I think we ought to hear from

Professor Foster. He has been working with our best people."

THE PRESIDENT: "Why in hell isn't Billy here?"

THE SECRETARY OF DEFENSE: "We might as well hear it from Professor Foster. If his statement is short, he can read it again for Billy."

THE PRESIDENT: "All right. But he reads it again for Billy."

(*The door opens. Enter Billy.*)

BILLY: "Greetings, everyone. God bless you all."

THE ATTORNEY GENERAL: "Are you sure you speak for Him?"

THE PRESIDENT: "Professor Foster has a statement. He has been meeting for the past week with my ad hoc committee of scientists. Would you read your statement, Professor?"

PROFESSOR FOSTER: "Here is our statement. In spite of all our efforts, we cannot ascertain the source of the signal."

THE PRESIDENT: "Is that all?"

PROFESSOR FOSTER: "Yes, sir. That's all."

THE ATTORNEY GENERAL: "Well, damn it to hell, sir, you must know where the signal comes from. Does it come from outer space? From the earth? From Russia?"

PROFESSOR FOSTER: "I stand by my statement."

THE PRESIDENT: "Well, here we are, faced with a show cause order. Billy, I don't expect anything from the Russians or the Chinese. Can we show cause?"

BILLY: "I have been thinking about that."

THE PRESIDENT: "Yes or no?"

(*Silence.*)

JERUSALEM

THE PRIME MINISTER: "At the suggestion of Professor Goldberg, I have invited Rabbi Cohen to this meeting."

THE FOREIGN MINISTER: "Why? To complicate this hoax?"

THE PRIME MINISTER: "Suppose we hear from Professor Goldberg."

PROFESSOR GOLDBERG: "Not only have we been working on it day and night, but we have been in touch with the Americans. As in our case, they can find no source for the signal. I think we ought to hear from Rabbi Cohen."

THE PRIME MINISTER: "What the Gentiles will do, Rabbi, is their problem. Ours is more personal, since when you come right down to it, our people have been faced with this problem before. We are presented with a show cause order. Can we show cause?"

RABBI COHEN: *(sadly)* "I am afraid not."

WHITEHALL

CHIEF OF INTELLIGENCE: "I've put four of our best men on it. We're running them north of the Afghan border."

THE PRIME MINISTER: "What do you hear from them?"

CHIEF OF INTELLIGENCE: "We've lost touch with them."

THE PRIME MINISTER: "I think you ought to get in touch with the Archbishop."

CHIEF OF INTELLIGENCE: "I'll put one of my best men on it."

(Thoughtful silence.)

THE VATICAN

FIRST CARDINAL: "I can't believe it. After two thousand years of effort."

SECOND CARDINAL: "Backbreaking effort."

FIRST CARDINAL: "No word of appreciation. Just show cause."

SECOND CARDINAL: "Have you spoken to the legal depart-
    ment?"
FIRST CARDINAL: "Oh, yes—yes indeed. He's within His
    rights, you know."

The above excerpts are just a sampling of what went on
in the upper circles of every government on earth. Both
the Vatican and Israel, due to the singular nature of their
antecedents, attempted to probe for a time limit, and at
least four times they were given the use of the broadcasting facilities of the Voice of America, both medium wave
and short wave; but their frantic pleas of "How much time
do we have?" were simply ignored. Day after day the resonant and majestic voice, same hour, same minute, called
upon the people of the earth to show cause.

By the third week, Russia and China and their client
countries joined in a public statement, denouncing the
voice as a tasteless bourgeois prank, directed at the moral
integrity of the peace-loving nations; and while they admitted that the source of the signal was not yet apparent,
they stated that it was only a matter of time before they
pinned it down. But Moscow's efforts to jam the voice continued to result in failure, and China finally accused Moscow of being a part of the Western conspiracy to foist their
primitive and anthropomorphic concept of a Biblical God
upon the civilized world.

Meanwhile, the various sectors of the human race reacted
in the entire spectrum of reaction, from hooting disdain
to indifference to anger and to riot and panic; and the
President of the United States had a long and earnest talk
in his study with his friend, Billy. Knowing only the results of this talk, one has to deduce its content, but one
can safely presume that it went somewhat in this fashion:

"I've read your bill of particulars, Billy. It's not very
convincing," the President said.

"No? Well, I didn't think too highly of it myself."

"I think you could have done better."

"Oh? Perhaps. Perhaps not. I never liked show cause orders—I was never wholly convinced that they are constitutional."

"They're constitutional," the President assured him. "I had a long talk with the Chief Justice about this. He says it's quite constitutional."

"I meant in a general sense. We must not become too parochial about this."

"One falls into the habit," the President confessed. "You must admit that we've always been on God's side."

"The question is—is He on our side?"

"You're not losing faith, Billy?"

"It's just the problem of making a case for us."

"He must be on our side," the President insisted. "Take the very fact of show cause. Our country has pioneered the legal field in the use of show cause orders. We were putting an end to subversive strikes with show cause orders before the rest of the world even thought of the device. And as far as a case for us—where else in the world has a nation provided as free and abundant a life as the American way?"

"I'm not sure that's to the point."

"Billy, I've never seen you like this before. I would have said you're the most confident man on earth. Do you want me to take this out of your hands and give it to the Attorney General? He has a damn good legal staff, and if they put their heads together, they'll come up with something that will hold up in court."

"That's not it. He asks a question point-blank. It's a moment of truth."

"We've had our moments of truth before, and we've lived through them."

"This one's different."

"Why?"

Billy looked at the President, and the President looked at Billy, and after a long, long moment of silence, the President nodded.

"Hopeless?"

"I thought of something," Billy said.

"What? I'll put every resource of the country at your disposal."

"When you come right down to it," Billy said, "it's the showing cause that breaks our back. It's one thing to preach in the big stadium at Houston; but when you say your piece at the United Nations, for example, it doesn't hold water."

"The hell it doesn't."

"Well, with England and Guatemala, but where's the plain majority we had ten years ago?"

"We're no worse than any other country and a damn sight better than the Reds."

"That's the crux of it," Billy said.

"You said you thought of something."

"I did. Let's take that big computer you have down at Houston. Suppose we start programming it. We'll throw everything into it, the good and the bad—get the best men in the field to program it, and keep throwing facts into it—say for a week or ten days."

"We don't know how much time we have."

"We have to presume that He knows what we're doing. And so long as He knows that we're working on the show cause order, He'll wait."

"Isn't that a calculated risk, Billy?"

"I'd say it's more of an educated guess. Good heavens, He's got all the time in the world. He invented it."

"Then why don't we bring IBM into it? They can throw together a set of computers that will make the thing down in Texas—that's where the big one is—look like a kiddy toy."

"If the government will foot the bill. I'm not sure that the IBM folk will see it just our way."

More or less in that fashion the IBM project came into being. Since they had a free hand to call on their own computer centers as well as what they had set up for the Department of Defense, it was no more than two weeks before they began the programming. Day and night, facts were fed into the giant complex of computers, day after day, not by a single person but by over three hundred computer experts; and precisely thirty-three days after they began, the job was done. The computer complex was the repository of all the facts available concerning the current role of the human species on the planet Earth.

It was three o'clock in the morning when the last fact was fed into the humming machine. At Central Control, a sleepless President and his Cabinet and some two dozen local luminaries and representatives of foreign countries waited. Billy waited with them. And the world waited.

"Well, Billy?" the President asked.

"We've given it the problem and the facts. Now we want the answer." He turned to the Chief Engineer of IBM. "It's your move now."

The Chief Engineer nodded and touched a button. The gigantic complex of computers came alive and hummed and throbbed and blinked and flashed, took a full sixty seconds to digest the information that had been fed to it, and then took ten seconds more to imprint the information on a piece of tape.

No one moved.

The President looked at Billy.

"It's up to you, sir," Billy said.

The President moved slowly toward the machine, tore off the six inches of tape that protruded from it, read it, then turned to Billy and handed it to him silently.

On the tape was printed: "Harvey Titterson."

"Harvey Titterson," Billy said.

The Attorney General came over and took the tape from Billy. "Harvey Titterson," he repeated.

"Harvey Titterson," the President said. "A billion dollars into the biggest computer project the world ever saw, and what do we have?"

"Harvey Titterson," said the Secretary of State.

"Who is Harvey Titterson?" asked the British Ambassador.

Who indeed? Two hours later the President of the United States and his friend, Billy, sat in the White House, facing the bulldog visage of the aging director of the Federal Bureau of Investigation.

"Harvey Titterson," said the President. "We want you to find him."

"Who is he?" asked the aging director of the Federal Bureau of Investigation.

"If we knew who he was, you would not have to find him," the President explained slowly and respectfully, for he was always respectful when he exchanged ideas with the aging director of the Federal Bureau of Investigation.

"Is he dangerous? Do we take him alive or dead?"

"You don't take him, sir," Billy explained respectfully, for like everyone else, he was always respectful when he spoke to the aging director of the Federal Bureau of Investigation. "We simply want to know where he is. If possible, we don't want him to be alarmed or disturbed in any way; as a matter of fact, we would prefer that he should be unaware of any special supervision. We only desire to know who he is and where he is."

"Have you looked in the telephone book?"

"We've been in touch with the telephone company," the President replied. "You must understand, we had no intention of bypassing you. But knowing the heavy load of work your department carries, we thought the telephone company might be able to simplify our task. Harvey Titterson does not have a telephone."

"It might be an unlisted number."

"No. The telephone company was very cooperative. It's not even an unlisted number."

"You'll have results, Mr. President," said the aging director of the Federal Bureau of Investigation. "I'll put two hundred of my best agents on it."

"Time is of the essence."

"Yes, sir. Time is of the essence."

It is a tribute to the Federal Bureau of Investigation and to the acumen of its aging director that in three days a report was placed upon the President's desk. The folder was marked "Confidential, top secret, restricted and special to the President of the United States."

The President called Billy into his office before he even opened the folder. "Billy," he said grimly, "this is your dish of tea. I've dealt with Russia and with Red China, but this is a piece of diplomacy you have to make your own. We'll read it together."

Then he opened the folder, and they read:

"Special secret report on Harvey Titterson, age twenty-two, son of Frank Titterson and Mary (Bently) Titterson. Born in Plainfield, New Jersey. Educated at Plainfield High School and at the University of California at Berkeley. Majored in Philosophy. Arrested twice for possession of marijuana. Sentence suspended in the first instance. Thirty days in jail in the second instance. Presently living at 921 East Eighth Street in New York City. Present occupation unknown."

"So that's Harvey Titterson," the President said. "He works in strange ways."

"I wouldn't blame Him," said Billy. "Harvey Titterson came out of the IBM machine."

"I want you to take this, Billy," the President said. "I

want you to carry on from here. I have given you top clearance. *Airforce 1* is at your disposal if you need it. Also my personal helicopter. It's your mission, and I don't have to say what rides on its success or failure."

"I'll do my best," Billy promised.

Two hours later a chauffeur-driven black government limousine drew up in front of 921 East Eighth Street, an old-law cold-water tenement, and Billy got out of the car, climbed four flights of stairs, and tapped at the door.

"Enter, brother," said a voice.

Billy opened the door and entered a room whose contents consisted of a table, a chair, a single bed, a rug, and on the rug a young man in ancient blue jeans and a T-shirt, sitting cross-legged. He had a russet beard and moustache, russet hair that fell to his shoulders, and a pair of bright blue eyes; and Billy couldn't help noticing his resemblance to his own mentor.

Billy stared at the young man, who stared back and said pleasantly, "You're sure as hell not fuzz and you're not the landlord, so you got to have the wrong place."

"Are you Harvey Titterson?" Billy asked.

"Right on. At least there are times when I believe I am. The search for identity is no simple matter."

Then Billy identified himself, and the young man grinned appreciatively. "Man, you are with it," he said.

"Let me come to the point," said Billy, "because time is of the essence. I have come to you on the question of our basic dilemma."

"You mean the war in Vietnam?"

"No, I mean the show cause order."

"Man, you confuse me. What show cause order?"

"Don't you read the newspapers?" Billy asked in amazement.

"Never."

"Surely you listen to radio—to television?"

"Don't own one."

"You meet people. At work. Everyone's talking—"

"I don't work."

"What do you do?"

"Man, you're direct," said Harvey Titterson. "I smoke a little grass and I meditate."

"How do you live?"

"Affluent parents. They tolerate me."

"But this has been going on for weeks. Surely you've been out of here?"

"I been on a long meditation trip."

"Are you a Jesus Freak?" Billy asked, drawing on his knowledge of the vernacular, a note of respect in his voice.

"No, hardly. I got my own way."

"Then let me bring you up to date. Some weeks ago, at precisely the same time all over the world, a voice took over the major broadcasting channels and spoke these words: 'You must show cause why the people of Earth shall not be destroyed. I am the Lord your God.' Those were the words."

"Cosmic," Harvey said. "Absolutely cosmic."

"It repeats every day. Same voice, same words."

"Absolutely cosmic."

"You can imagine the results," Billy said.

"It must have been a hassle."

"China, Russia—all over the world."

"Out of sight," said Harvey.

"The President is a friend of mine—"

"Oh?"

"The point is, I convinced him that there was no simple answer. He depends on me for this kind of thing. It's a great honor, but this was too big."

"Absolutely cosmic," Harvey said.

"So I came up with an idea and sold it to him. We put together the biggest computer the world ever saw, and we fed it all the information there is. Everything. And then, when we put the question to it, it came up with your name."

"You're putting me on."

"You have my word of honor, Harvey."

"That shakes me."

"So you see what it means to us, Harvey. You're the last hope. Can you show cause?"

"Heavy—very heavy."

"Maybe you want time to think about it?"

"You don't want to think about it," Harvey said. "If it's there, it's there."

"Is it there?"

Harvey Titterson closed his eyes for a long moment, and then he looked up at Billy and said simply:

"We are what we are."

"What?"

"We are what we are."

"Just that?"

"Man, it's your thing. Just think about it."

"Exodus three, fourteen," Billy said. " 'And God said unto Moses, I am what I am.' "

"Right on."

Billy looked at his watch. It was three minutes before eleven o'clock. With hardly a thank you, he bolted out of the room and down the stairs and into the big black limousine.

"Turn on the radio!" he shouted at the chauffeur. "Eight eighty on the dial."

The chauffeur fiddled nervously.

"Eight eighty—what's holding you?"

"This is the Columbia Broadcasting Company," the radio crackled, "CBS radio in New York City. At this time we have been leaving the air for a special announcement." Then silence. Silence. Minute after minute went by, and still silence.

Then the voice of the announcer, "Apparently we are not to be interrupted today—"

On the fourth floor of the tenement, Harvey Titterson rolled a joint, had a toke, and then laid it aside.

"Crazy," he said softly.

And then he composed himself to continue his meditation trip.

7
Not with a Bang

On the evening of the third of April, standing at the window of his pleasant three-bedroom, split-level house and admiring the sunset, Alfred Collins saw a hand rise above the horizon, spread thumb and forefinger, and snuff out the sun. It was the moment of soft twilight, and it ended as abruptly as if someone had flicked an electric switch.

Which is precisely what his wife did. She put on lights all over the house. "My goodness, Al," she said, "it did get dark quickly, didn't it?"

"That's because someone snuffed out the sun."

"What on earth are you talking about?" she asked. "And by the way, the Bensons are coming for dinner and bridge tonight, so you'd better get dressed."

"All right. You weren't watching the sunset, were you?"

"I have other things to do."

"Yes. Well, what I mean is that if you were watching, you would have seen this hand come up behind the hori-

zon, and then the thumb and the forefinger just spread
out, and then they came together and snuffed out the
sun."

"Really. Now for heaven's sake, Al, don't redouble
tonight. If you are doubled, have faith in your bad bidding. Do you promise me?"

"Funniest damn thing about the hand. It brought back
all my childhood memories of anthropomorphism."

"And just what does that mean?"

"Nothing. Nothing at all. I'm going to take a shower."

"Don't be all evening about it."

At dinner, Al Collins asked Steve Benson whether he
had been watching the sunset that evening.

"No—no, I was showering."

"And you, Sophie?" Collins asked of Benson's wife.

"No way. I was changing a hem. What does women's
lib intend to do about hems? There's the essence of the
status of women, the nitty-gritty of our servitude."

"It's one of Al's jokes," Mrs. Collins explained. "He
was standing at the window and he saw this hand come
over the horizon and snuff out the sun."

"Did you, Al?"

"Scout's honor. The thumb and forefinger parted, then
came together. Poof. Out went the sun."

"That's absolutely delicious," Sophie said. "You have
such delicious imagination."

"Especially in his bidding," his wife remarked.

"She'll never forget that slam bid doubled and re-
doubled," Sophie said. It was evident that she would never
forget it either.

"Interesting but impractical," said Steve Benson, who
was an engineer at IBM. "You're dealing with a body that
is almost a million miles in diameter. The internal tem-
perature is over ten million degrees centigrade, and at its
core the hydrogen atoms are reduced to helium ash. So

all you have is poetic symbolism. The sun will be here for a long time."

After the second rubber, Sophie Benson remarked that either it was chilly in the Collins house or she was catching something.

"Al, turn up the thermostat," said Mrs. Collins.

The Collins team won the third and fourth rubbers, and Mrs. Collins had all the calm superiority of a winner as she bid her guests good night. Al Collins went out to the car with them, thinking that, after all, suburban living was a strange process of isolation and alienation. In the city, a million people must have watched the thing happen; here, Steve Benson was taking a shower and his wife was changing a hem.

It was a very cold night for April. Puddles of water left over from a recent rain had frozen solid, and the star-drenched sky had the icy look of midwinter. Both of the Bensons had arrived without coats, and as they hurried into their car, Benson laughingly remarked that Al was probably right about the sun. Benson had difficulty starting the car, and Al Collins stood shivering until they had driven away. Then he looked at the outside thermometer. It was down to sixteen degrees.

"Well, we beat them loud and clear," his wife observed when he came back to the house. He helped her clean up, and while they were at it, she asked him just what he meant by anthropomorphism or whatever it was.

"It's a sort of primitive notion. You know, the Bible says that God made man in His own image."

"Oh? You know, I absolutely believed it when I was a child. What are you doing?"

He was at the fireplace, and he said that he thought he'd build a fire.

"In April? You must be out of your mind. Anyway, I cleaned the hearth."

"I'll clean it up tomorrow."

"Well, I'm going to bed. I think you're crazy to start a fire at this time of the night, but I'm not going to argue with you. This is the first time you did not overbid, and thank heavens for small favors."

The wood was dry, and the fire was warm and pleasant to watch. Collins had never lost his pleasure at watching the flames of a fire, and he mixed himself a long scotch and water, and sat in front of the flames, sipping the drink and recalling his own small scientific knowledge. The green plants would die within a week, and after that the oxygen would go. How long? he wondered. Two days—ten days—he couldn't remember and he had no inclination to go to the encyclopedia and find out. It would get very cold, terribly cold. It surprised him that instead of being afraid, he was only mildly curious.

He looked at the thermometer again before he went to bed. It was down to zero now. In the bedroom, his wife was already asleep, and he undressed quietly and put an extra comforter on the bed before he crawled in next to her. She moved toward him, and feeling her warm body next to him, he fell asleep.

8
A Talent
of Harvey

Harvey Kepplemen never knew that he had a talent for anything, until one Sunday morning at breakfast he plucked a crisp water roll right out of the air.

It balanced the universe; it steadied the order of things. Man is man, and particularly in this age of equality, when uniformity has become both a passion and a religion, it would be unconscionable that a decent human being of forty years should have no talent at all. Yet Harvey Kepplemen was so obviously and forthrightly an untalented man—until this morning—that the label was pinned on him descriptively. As one says, He is short, She is fat, He is handsome, so they would say of Harvey: Nothing there. No talent. No verve. Pale. Colorless. No bent. No aptitude. He was a quiet, soft-spoken person of middle height, with middling looks and brown eyes and brown hair that was thinning in a moderately even manner, and he had passable teeth with good fillings and clean fingernails, and he was an accountant with an income of eighteen thousand dollars a year.

Just that. He was not given to anger, moods, or depression, and if any observer had cared to observe him, he would have said that Harvey was a cheerful enough person; except that one never noticed whether he was cheerful or not. Suzie was his wife. Suzie's mother once put the question to her. "Is Harvey always so cheerful?" Suzie's mother wanted to know.

"Cheerful? I never think of Harvey as being cheerful."

Neither did anyone else, but that was because no one ever gave any serious thought to Harvey. Perhaps if there had been children, they might have had opinions concerning their father; but it was a childless marriage. Not an unhappy one, not a very happy one. Simply childless.

Nevertheless, Suzie was quite content. Small, dark, reasonably attractive, she accepted Harvey. Neither of them was rebellious. Life was just the way it was. Sunday morning was just the way it was. They slept late but not too late. They had brunch at precisely eleven o'clock. Suzie prepared toast, two eggs for each of them, three slices of crisp bacon for each of them, orange juice to begin and coffee to finish. She also set out two jars of jam, imported marmalade, which Harvey liked, and grape jelly, which she liked.

On this Sunday morning, Harvey thought that he would have liked a crisp roll.

"Really?" Suzie said. "I never knew that you liked rolls particularly. You do like toast."

"Oh, yes," Harvey agreed. "I do like toast."

"I mean, we always have toast."

"I have toast for lunch, too, "Harvey agreed.

"I could have bought rolls."

"I don't think so, because I guess I was thinking about the kind of rolls we had when I was a kid. They were very light and crisp, and they were two for a nickel. Can you imagine paying only a nickel for two rolls?"

"No. Really, I can't."

"Well, no more light, crisp water rolls, two for a nickel." Harvey sighed. "Wouldn't it be nice if I could just reach up like this and pluck one out of the air?"

And then Harvey reached up and plucked a crisp, brown water roll right out of the air, and sat there, arm frozen into position, mouth open, staring at the water roll; then he lowered his arm slowly and placed the roll on the table in front of him and continued to stare at it.

"That's very clever, Harvey," Suzie said. "Is it a surprise for me? I think you did it perfectly."

"Did what?"

"You plucked that roll right out of the air." Suzie picked up the roll. "It's warm—really, you are clever, Harvey." She broke it open and tasted it. "So good! Where did you buy it, Harvey?"

"What?"

"The roll. I hope you bought another one."

"What roll?"

"This one."

"Where did it come from?"

"Harvey, you just plucked it right out of the air. Do you remember the magician who entertained at Lucy Gordon's party? He did it with white doves. But I think you did it just as nicely with the roll, and it's such a surprise, because I can imagine how much you practiced."

"I didn't practice."

"Harvey!"

"Did I really take that roll out of the air?"

"You did, Mr. Magician," Suzie said proudly. She had a delicious feeling of pride, a very new feeling. While she had never been ashamed of Harvey before, she had certainly never been proud of him.

"I don't know how I did it."

"Oh, Harvey, stop putting me on. I am terribly impressed. Really, I am."

Harvey reached out, broke off a piece of the roll, and tasted it. It was quite good, fresh, straightforward, honest bread, precisely like the two-for-a-nickel rolls he had eaten as a child.

"Put some butter on it," Suzie suggested.

Harvey buttered his piece and then topped it with marmalade. He licked his lips with appreciation. Suzie poured him another cup of coffee.

Harvey finished the roll—Suzie refusing any more than a taste—and then he shook his head thoughtfully. "Damned funny," he said. "I just reached up and took it out of the air."

"Oh, Harvey."

"That's what I did. That's exactly what I did."

"Your eggs are getting cold," Suzie reminded him.

He shook his head. "No—it couldn't have happened that way. Then where did it come from?"

"Do you want me to put them back in the pan?"

"Listen, Suzie. Now just listen to me. I got to thinking about those rolls I ate when I was a kid, and I said to myself, wouldn't it be nice to have one right now, and wouldn't it be nice just to reach up and pick it out of the air—like this." And suiting his action to the thought, he plucked another roll out of the air and dropped it on the table like a hot coal.

"See what I mean?"

Suzie clapped her hands. "Wonderful! Beautiful! I was staring right at you and I never saw you do it."

Harvey picked up the second roll. "I didn't do it," he said bleakly. "I haven't been practicing sleight of hand. You know me, Suzie. I can't do the simplest card trick."

"That's what makes it so wonderful—because you had all these hidden qualities and you brought them out."

"No—no. Remember how it is when we play poker, Suzie, and it's my deal, and it's a great big yak because I can't shuffle the cards, and it's the big laugh of the evening when I try it and the cards are all over the table. You don't unlearn something like that."

Suzie's eyes widened, and for the first time she realized that her husband was sitting at the table in a T-shirt, with no sleeves and no equipment other than two cold eggs and three strips of bacon.

"Harvey, you mean—"

"I mean," he said. "Yes."

"But from where? Gettleson's Bakery is four blocks away."

"They don't make water rolls at Gettleson's Bakery."

They sat in silence then and stared at each other.

"Maybe it's something you have a talent for," Suzie said finally.

More silence.

"Do you suppose it's only rolls?" Suzie said. "I mean just rolls? Suppose you tried a Danish?"

"I don't like Danish," Harvey answered miserably.

"You like the kind with the prune filling. I mean, when they're crisp and have a lot of prune filling and they're not all that limp, squishy kind of dough."

"You don't get them like that anymore."

"Well, you remember when we drove down to Washington, and we stopped at that motel outside of Baltimore, and you remember how they told us they had their own chef who worked in one of the big hotels in Germany, only he wasn't a Nazi or anything like that, and he made the Danish himself and you remember how much you liked it. So you could just think about that kind of Danish, full of prune filling."

Harvey thought about it. His hand was shaking as he reached out to a spot midway between himself and Suzie, and there it was between his thumb and his forefinger, a piece of Danish so impossibly full of sweet prune filling that it almost came to pieces in Harvey's fingers. He let it plop down on the cold eggs.

"Oh—you've spoiled the eggs," Suzie said.

"Well, they were cold anyway."

"Yes, I suppose so. I can make you some fresh eggs."

Harvey put a finger into the prune filling and then licked it thoughtfully. He broke off a corner of the Danish, ignoring the cold egg yellow that adhered, and munched it.

"There's no use making fresh eggs," Suzie observed, "because now that sweet stuff will ruin your appetite. Is it good?"

"Delicious."

Then, in a squeak that was almost a scream, Suzie demanded to know where the Danish came from.

"You saw it. You told me to get a Danish."

"Oh, my God, Harvey!"

"That's the way I feel about it. It's damn funny, isn't it?"

"You took that Danish right out of the air."

"That's what I've been trying to tell you."

"It wasn't a trick," said Suzie. "I think I am going to be sick, Harvey. I think I am going to throw up."

She rose and went to the bathroom, and Harvey listened unhappily to the sound of the toilet being flushed. Then she brushed her teeth. They were both of them very clean and neat people. When she returned to the breakfast table, she had gotten a grip on herself, and she told Harvey matter-of-factly that she had read an article in the magazine section of *The New York Times* to the effect that all so-called miracles and religious phenomena of the past were simply glossed-over scientific facts, totally comprehensible in the light of present-day knowledge.

"Would you repeat that please, darling?" Harvey asked her.

"I mean that the Danish must have come from somewhere."

"Baltimore," Harvey agreed.

"Do you want to try something else?" she asked tentatively.

"No. I don't think so."

"Then I think we ought to call my brother, Dave."

"Why?"

"Because," Suzie said, "and I don't want to hurt your feelings, Harvey, but simply because Dave knows what to do."

"About what?"

"I know you don't like Dave—"

Dave was heavy, overbearing, arrogant, insensitive, and contemptuous of Harvey.

"I don't like him very much," Harvey admitted. Harvey disliked feelings of hostility toward anyone. "I can get along with him," he added. "I mean, Suzie, you cannot imagine how much I try to like Dave because he is your brother, but whenever I approach him—"

"Harvey," she interrupted, "I know." Then she telephoned Dave.

Dave always had three eggs for breakfast. Harvey sat at the table and watched gloomily as Dave stuffed himself and Dave's wife, Ruthie, explained about Dave's digestion. Dave had never taken a laxative. "Dave has a motto," Ruthie explained. "You are what you eat."

"The brain needs food, the body needs food," Dave agreed. "What kind of trouble are you in, Harvey? You're upset. You're down. When I see a man who's down, I know the whole story. Up and down, which is the secret of life, Harvey. It's as simple as that. Up. As simple as that. You got any more bacon, Suzie?"

Suzie brought the bacon to the table, sat down, and

carefully explained what had happened that morning. Dave grinned but did not stop eating.

"I don't think you understood me," Suzie said.

Dave cleared his mouth, chewed firmly, and congratulated the Kepplemens. "Ruthie," he said, "how many times have I said to you, the trouble with Harvey and Suzie is they got no sense of humor? How many times?"

"Maybe fifty times," Ruthie replied amiably.

"It's not the biggest shtick in the world," Dave said charitably. "But it's cute. Harvey takes things out of the air. It's all right."

"Not things. Water rolls and a piece of Danish."

"What are water rolls?" Ruthie wanted to know.

"They're a kind of roll," Harvey explained uncomfortably. "They used to make them when I was a kid. Crisp outside and soft inside."

"Here is half of the second one," Suzie said, handing it to Ruthie. Ruthie examined it and nibbled tentatively. "You remember the way Pop used to dip his water rolls into the coffee," Suzie said to Dave.

"You got to butter it first," Dave told Ruthie. "Go ahead, try it."

"You don't believe one word I have said." Suzie turned to her husband. "Go ahead, Harvey. Show them."

Harvey shook his head.

"Come on, Harvey—come on," Dave said. "One lousy roll. What have you got to lose?"

For the first time that morning, Harvey felt good, really good. He reached across the table and from the airspace directly in front of his brother-in-law's nose he extracted a warm, crisp brown roll, held it for a long moment, and then placed it on Dave's plate.

"Oh, my God!" Ruthie cried.

Suzie grinned with delight, and Dave, his mouth open,

stared at the roll and said nothing. He just stared and said nothing.

"It's still warm. Eat it," Harvey said with authority. It was possibly the first thing he had ever said to Dave with any kind of authority.

Dave shook his head.

Harvey broke open the roll and buttered it, the butter melting on the hot white bread. He handed it to Dave, and Dave nibbled at it tentatively. "Not bad, not bad." Dave took two large bites. He was beginning to be himself again. "You're not crapping around, are you, Harvey?" he asked. "No—no, it's impossible. You're the clumsiest jerk that ever tried to shuffle a deck of cards, so how could it be sleight of hand? Then what is it, Harvey?"

Harvey shook his head hopelessly.

"It's a gift," Suzie said.

"Did you feel it coming on, Harvey?" Dave wanted to know. "I mean, did it grow on you—or what?"

"Is it only rolls?" Ruthie asked.

"Also Danish," Suzie said.

"What's Danish?"

"Danish pastry with prune filling."

"I got to see that," Dave said, and then Harvey took a Danish out of the air. Dave stared and nodded, and he took a bite of the Danish. "Just rolls and Danish?"

"That's all I tried."

A slow, crafty grin spread over Dave's face as he reached into his pocket and took out a roll of bills. He peeled off a ten-dollar bill and pressed it flat on the table. "You know what this is, Harvey?"

Harvey stared at it without comment.

"How about it?"

"It could get us into a lot of trouble," Harvey said thoughtfully.

"How?"

"Counterfeit."

"Come off it, Harvey. What's counterfeit? Are you counterfeiting rolls? Danish?"

"Rolls are different. This is larceny, Dave."

The two ladies listened and watched, their eyes wide, but said nothing. Morality had reared its ugly head, and suddenly what had been very simple was becoming most complicated.

"There never was an accountant who didn't have larceny in him. Come on, Harvey."

Harvey shook his head.

"It's a gift," Suzie explained. "It's spooky. I don't think you should talk Harvey into doing anything that he doesn't want to do. You don't want to do this, do you, Harvey?" she asked her husband. "I mean, unless you really want to."

"Listen, Harvey, level with me," Dave said. "Did you ever do anything like this before? Have you been working up to this?"

"How do you work up to it?"

"That's what I'm asking you. Because this is big—big, Harvey. If it's just a gift, you know, all of a sudden, then you got no obligations to anyone. You can take Danish out of the air. You can take a ten-dollar bill out of the air. What's the difference?"

"Counterfeit," said Harvey.

"Balls. Are the rolls counterfeit, or are they the real thing?"

"It's still counterfeiting."

"Harvey, you are out of your ever-loving mind. Look, you're sitting here in the bosom of your family—those closest to you, your own loved ones. You're protected. Suzie is your wife. I'm her brother. Ruthie is my wife.

Flesh and blood. Who's going to turn you in? Myself— would I kill the goose that laid the golden egg? Ruthie— I'd break every bone in her body."

"That's right, he would," Ruthie said eagerly. "I can promise you that, Harvey. He would break every bone in my body."

"Suzie? Suzie, would you turn Harvey in? Like hell you would. A wife can't testify against her husband. That's what I have been telling you, Harvey. Flesh and blood."

"When you think about it," Suzie said, "it's just like a parlor game, Harvey. I mean, suppose we were playing Monopoly or something like that. I mean, if you just did it for laughs. Dave says, take a ten-dollar bill out of the air. You do it. So what?"

"Maybe a dollar bill," Harvey said, for the arguments were very convincing.

"Right on," said Dave, taking a dollar bill out of his pocket. "I should have thought of that myself, Harv. Today a dollar is worth nothing. nothing. It's like a gag." He spread the dollar on the table. "You know, when I was a kid, this could buy something. Not today. No, sir."

Harvey nodded, took a deep breath, reached for a spot two feet in front of his nose, and plucked a dollar bill out of the air. Suzie squealed with pleasure and Ruthie clapped her hands in delight. Dave grinned and took the dollar bill from Harvey, laid it on the table next to the one he had produced from his pocket, and scrutinized it carefully. Then he shook his head.

"You missed, Harvey."

"What do you mean, I missed?"

"Well, it's sort of a dollar bill. You got Washington's face all right, and it says 'one dollar,' but the color's not exactly right, it's too green—"

"You left out the little print," Ruthie exclaimed. "Here

where it says that it's legal tender for all debts, public and private—you left that out."

Harvey could see the difference. The curlicues were different, and the bright green stamp of the Department of the Treasury was the same color as the rest of it. The serial numbers had been left out, and as for the reverse side, it bore only a general resemblance to a real dollar bill.

"OK, OK—don't get nervous," Dave told him. "You couldn't be expected to hit it the first time. What you have to do is to take a real good look at the genuine article and then try it again."

"I'd rather not."

"Come on, Harv—come on. Don't chicken out now. You want to try a ten?"

"No, I'll try the one again."

He reached into the air and returned with another dollar bill between his fingers. They all examined it eagerly.

"Good, good," Dave said. "Not perfect, Harvey—you missed on the seal, and the paper's not right. But it's better. I'll bet I could pass this one."

"No!" Harvey grabbed both spurious bills and stuffed them into his pocket.

"All right, all right—don't blow your cool, Harv. We try it again now."

"No."

"What do you mean, no?"

"No. I'm tired. Anyway, I got to think about this. I'm half out of my mind the way it is. Suppose this happened to you?"

"Man oh man, I'd buy General Motors before the week was out."

"Well, I'm not sure that I want to buy General Motors or anything else. I got to think about this."

"Harvey's right," Suzie put in. "You always come on

too strong, Dave. Harvey's got a right to think about this."

"And while he thinks, the gift goes."

"How do you know?"

"Well, it came on sudden. Suppose it goes the same way?"

"I don't care if it does," Suzie said loyally. "Harvey's got a right to think about it."

"OK. I'm not going to be unreasonable. Only one thing —when he thinks his way out of this, I want you to call me. I'm going to get some twenties and some fifties. I don't think we should go in for anything bigger than that right now."

"I'll call you."

"OK. Just remember that."

When Dave and Ruthie had departed, Harvey asked his wife why she had agreed to call. "I don't need Dave," he said. "You and Dave treat me like an imbecile."

"I just agreed to get rid of him."

"I'd just like to think once that you were on my side and not on his."

"That's not fair. I'm always on your side. You know that."

"I don't know it."

"All right, make a big federal case out of it. They're gone, so if you want to think about it, why don't you think about it?" And she stalked into the bedroom, slammed the door, and turned on the television.

Harvey sat in the living room and brooded. He took out the dollar bills, studied them for a while, and then tore them up and made a trip to the bathroom to flush them down the drain. Then he returned to the couch and brooded again. It had been late afternoon by the time Dave and Ruthie left, and now it was early in the evening and darkening, and he was beginning to be hungry. He went into the kitchen and found beer and bread and

ham, but his inner yearning was for a hamburger sandwich, not the way Suzie made hamburgers, dry, tasteless,
leathery, but tender and juicy and pink in the middle.
Reflecting on the fact that he was married to a rotten
cook, he took a hamburger sandwich out of the air. It
was perfect. Suzie entered as he took his first bite.

"Don't think about me," she said. "I could starve to
death while you sit here stuffing yourself."

"Since when do I let you starve to death?"

"Where did you get the hamburger?"

He took one out of the air and put it in front of her.

"It's full of onions," Suzie said. "You know how I hate
onions."

Harvey rose and dropped the hamburger into the garbage pail.

"Harvey, what are you doing?"

"You don't like onions."

"Well, you can't just throw it away."

"Why not?" Harvey felt himself changing, and the
change was encompassed in those two simple words—why
not? Why not? He plucked a hamburger without onions
out of the air, dry and hard, the way his wife cooked them.

"Be my guest," he said coolly.

She took a bite of the hamburger and then informed
him through a mouth filled with food that he was acting
very funny.

"What do you mean, funny?"

"You're just acting funny, Harvey. You got to admit
that you are acting funny."

"All right, it's a different situation."

"What do you mean?"

"I mean, I can take things out of the air," said Harvey.
"That's pretty different. I mean, it's not something that
you go around doing. For example, you want some chocolate cake?" He reached out and retrieved a piece of

chocolate layer cake and placed it in front of Suzie. "How does it taste? Try it."

"Harvey, I'm still eating the hamburger, and don't think I don't realize that it's very unusual what you can do."

"It's not like I'm just a kid," Harvey said. "I'm a forty-one-year-old loser."

"You're not a loser, Harvey."

"Don't you kid yourself. I am a loser. What have we got? Five thousand dollars in the bank, a four-room apartment, no kids, nothing, absolutely nothing, a great big fat zero, and I am still forty-one years old."

"I don't like to hear you talk like that, Harvey."

"I am just making the point that I got to think this through. I got to get used to the fact that I can take things out of the air. It's an unusual talent. I got to convince myself."

"Why? Don't you believe it, Harvey?"

"I do and I don't. That's why I have to think about it."

Suzie nodded. "I understand." She ate the chocolate cake and then went into the bedroom and turned on the television again.

Harvey followed her into the bedroom. "Why do you say you understand? Why do you always tell me that you understand?" She was trying to concentrate on the television screen, and she shook her head. "Will you turn off that damn box!" Harvey shouted.

"Don't shout at me, Harvey."

"Then listen to me. You watch me take things out of the air and tell me you understand. I take a piece of chocolate cake out of the air, and you tell me that you understand. I don't understand, but you tell me that you understand."

"That's the way it is, Harvey. They send people up to the moon, and I don't know any more about it than you do, but that's the way science is. I think it's very nice that you can take things out of the air. I think that if one of those computer places put it on a computer, they would be able to tell you just how it works."

"Then why do you keep saying that you understand?"

'I understand that you want to think about it. Why don't you sit down inside and think about it."

Harvey closed the door of the bedroom and went back into the living room and thought about it. It was actually the first moment he had really thought about it, and suddenly his head was exploding with ideas and notions. Some were what his friends in the advertising agencies would have called very creative notions, and some were not. Some were simply the crystallization of his own dissatisfactions. If someone had suggested to him the day before that he was a seething mass of dissatisfactions, he would have denied the accusation hotly. Now he could face them as facts. He was dissatisfied with his life, his job, his home, his past, his future, and his wife. He had never set out to be an accountant; it had simply happened to him. He had always dreamed of living in a large, spacious country home, and here he was in a miserable apartment with paper-thin walls in an enormous jerry-built building on Third Avenue in New York City. As far as his past was concerned, it was colorless and flat, and his future promised nothing that was much better. His wife—?

He thought about his wife. It was not that he disliked Suzie; he had nothing against her, nor could he think of very much that he had going for her. She was short, dark, and pretty, but he couldn't remember why or exactly how he had come to marry her. The plain fact of the matter was that he adored oversized blondes, large, tall, buxom, beautiful blondes. He dreamed about such women; he turned to watch them on the street; he fell asleep thinking about them and he awakened thinking about them.

He thought about one of them now. And then he began

to grin; an idea had clamped onto him and it wouldn't
let go. He sat up in his chair and stared at the bedroom
door. He straightened his spine. The television blared
from behind the door.

"To hell with it!" he said. It was a new Harvey Kepplemen. He stood up, his spine erect. "Tall, blond, beautiful—" he whispered, and then hesitated over the notion of
intelligence. "To hell with intelligence!"

He reached out into the air in front of him with both
hands now, and suddenly there she was, but he couldn't
hold her and she fell with an enormous thud and lay
sprawled on the floor, a blond, naked woman, very beautiful, very large, magnificently full-breasted, blue eyes wide
open and very motionless and apparently lifeless.

Harvey stood staring at her.

The bedroom door opened, and there was Suzie, who
also stood and stared at her.

"What is that?" Suzie cried out.

The answer was self-evident. Harvey swallowed, closed
his mouth, and bent over the beautiful blonde.

"Don't touch her!"

"Maybe she's dead," Harvey said hopelessly. "I got to
touch her to find out."

"Who is she? Where did she come from?"

Harvey turned to meet Suzie's eyes.

"No."

Harvey nodded.

"No. I don't believe it. That?" Now Suzie walked over
to the large blonde. "She's seven feet long if she's an inch.
Harvey, what kind of a creep are you?"

Harvey touched her, discreetly, on the chest just below
the enormous breasts. She was as cold as a dead mackerel.

"Well?"

"She's as cold as a dead mackerel," Harvey replied
bleakly.

"Try her pulse."

"She's dead. Look at her eyes." He tried the pulse. "She has no pulse."

"Great," Suzie said. "That's just great, Harvey. Here we are with a dead seven-foot-long blonde with oversized mammaries, and now what?"

"I think you ought to cover her up," Harvey suggested meekly.

"You're damn right I'm going to cover her up!" And Suzie marched off to the bedroom and returned with a blanket which just about fitted the enormous body.

"What do I do now?" Harvey wondered.

"Put her back where you got her from."

"You must be kidding."

"Try it," said a new Suzie, cold and nasty. "If you can take things like this out of the air, maybe you can put them back."

"How? Just suppose you tell me how, being such a great smart-ass about everything else."

"I'm not a prevert."

"You mean pervert. Who's a pervert? That's a hell of a thing to say."

Suzie swept the blanket aside. "Look at her."

"All right, I've seen her. Now what do we do with her?"

"What do *you* do."

"OK, OK—what do I do?"

"Lift her up and put her back."

"Where?"

"Wherever you take these damn things from, back with your lousy water rolls and Danish pastry."

Harvey shook his head. "We been married a long time, Suzie. I never heard you talk like that before."

"You never made me a present of a seven-foot dead blonde before."

"I guess not," Harvey agreed, reaching out and obtaining a prune Danish.

"What's that for?"

"I want to see if I can put it back."

"Look, Harvey," Suzie said, her voice softening a little, "it's no use putting back a prune Danish. You got to put back big Bertha there." Harvey, meanwhile, was stabbing the air with the prune Danish. "Harvey—forget the Danish."

He let go of it, hoping and praying that it would return to whatever unknown had produced it, but instead it dropped with a wet plop on one of the huge breasts, dripping its soft prune filling all over the beautiful oversized mammary. Harvey ran for a napkin, wiped frantically, and only made the situation worse. Suzie joined him with a wet sponge and a handful of paper towels.

"Let me do it, Harvey."

She cleaned up the mess while Harvey managed to heave one of the long, meaty legs into the air. "Put her back," he said. "Suzie, I could never lift her. It would take one of those hoist cranes. She must weigh two hundred and fifty pounds."

"I suppose that's what you always wanted. Do you know, she's as cold as ice."

"Do you suppose I killed her?" he asked woefully.

"I don't know. I think I'll telephone Dave."

"Why?"

"He'll know what to do."

"As far as I am concerned, your brother Dave can drop dead."

"Like this one. Sure. Wish me dead too."

"I never wished you dead. I am talking about your brother, Dave."

"At least he'd have an idea."

"So have I," Harvey said. "My idea is very simple and right on it. Call the cops."

"What? Harvey, are you out of your ever-loving mind? She's dead. You made her dead. You killed her."

"So I made her dead. What do we do? Cut her up and

flush her down the toilet? Neither of us can stand the sight of blood. Do we dump her in an empty lot? Even with your lousy brother Dave, we couldn't lift her up."

"Harvey," she pleaded, "let's think about it."

They thought about it, and then Harvey called the cops.

A dead body, Harvey discovered, was a communal enter-prise. Nine men prowled around the little apartment. Eight of them were ambulance attendants, uniformed of-ficers, fingerprint expert, medical examiner, photographer, etc. The ninth was a heavy-shouldered man in plain clothes, whose name was Lieutenant Serpio, who told everyone else what to do, and who never smiled. Harvey and Suzie sat on the couch and watched him.

"All right, take her out," said Serpio.

They tried.

"Never saw the like of it," the Medical Examiner was muttering. "She's seven feet tall if she's an inch."

"Kelly, don't stand there on your feet, give them a hand!" Serpio said to one of the uniformed cops.

Kelly joined with the ambulance attendants, and with the help of another cop they got the oversized blonde onto a stretcher. She hung over either end as they staggered through the door with her, and Suzie said to her husband:

"You're not a pervert, Harvey. You're just a lousy male chauvinist. I have been thinking about you. You are a sexist pig."

"That's great," Harvey agreed. "I never did anything to anyone, and the whole world falls on me."

"You are a sexist pig," she repeated.

"I find it hard to think of myself that way."

"Just try. You'll get used to it."

"What did she die from, Doc?" Lieutenant Serpio asked the Medical Examiner.

"God knows. Maybe she broke her back carrying that

bust around. I'll go downtown and chop her up a little, and I'll let you know."

The apartment cleared out. Only Serpio and a single uniformed cop remained. Serpio stood in front of Harvey and Suzie, staring at them thoughtfully.

"Tell me again," he said.

"I told you."

"Tell me again. I got plenty of time. In twenty years of practicing my profession in this town, I thought I had seen everything. Not so. This enlivens my work and gives me a new attitude. Now who is she?"

"I don't know."

"Where did she come from?"

"I took her out of the air."

"I know. You took her out of the air. I could send you down to Bellevue, only I am intrigued. Do you make a habit out of taking things out of the air?"

"No, sir," Harvey answered politely. "Only since this morning."

"What about you?" he said to Suzie. "Do you take hings out of the air?"

She shook her head. "It's Harvey's gift."

"What else does Harvey take out of the air?" the Lieutenant asked patiently.

"Danish."

"Danish?"

"Danish pastry with prune filling," Harvey explained.

The Lieutenant considered this. "I see. Tell me, Mr. Kepplemen, why Danish pastry with prune filling—if it's not too much to ask?"

"I can explain that," Suzie put in. "You see, we were down in Baltimore—"

"Let him explain."

"I like it," Harvey said.

"What about Baltimore?"

"They make it very good down there," Harvey said.

"Danish pastry?"

"Yes, sir."

"Now do you want to tell me who the blonde is?"

"I don't know."

"Do you want to tell me how she died?"

"I don't know."

"The doctor says she's been dead for hours. When did she come here?"

"I told you."

"Where are her clothes, Harvey?"

"I told you. I got her just the way she was."

"All right, Harvey," the Lieutenant said with a sigh. "I am going to have to arrest you and your wife and take you downtown, because with an explanation like this, I have absolutely no alternative. Now I am going to tell you your rights. No, the hell with that. Tell you what, Harvey —you and your wife come downtown with me, and we'll let the arrest sit for a while, and we'll see if the boys downstairs figured out what she died from. How does that grab you?"

Harvey and Suzie nodded bleakly.

On the way down to Centre Street, they sat in the back seat of Lieutenant Serpio's car and argued in whispers.

"Show him with a Danish," Suzie kept whispering.

"No."

"Why not?"

"I don't want to."

"Well, he doesn't believe you. That's plain enough. If you take out a Danish, maybe he'll believe you."

"No."

"A hamburger?"

"No."

Lieutenant Serpio led them into an office where there

were a lot of cops in uniform and some not in uniform, and he led them to a bench and said, with some solicitude, "Both of you sit down right here, and just take it easy and don't get nervous. You want anything, you ask that fella over there by the desk."

Then he went over to the desk and spoke softly to the cop behind it for a minute or so; and then the cop behind the desk came over to Suzie and Harvey and said, "Now just take it easy, and don't get nervous, and everything's going to be all right. You want a prune Danish, Harvey?"

"Why?"

"If you're hungry. Nothing to it. I send the kid out for it, and in five minutes you got a prune Danish. How about it?"

"No," replied Harvey.

"I think we ought to call our lawyer," said Suzie.

The cop went away, and Harvey asked her whom she expected to call, since they never had a lawyer.

"I don't know, Harvey. Somebody always calls a lawyer. I'm scared."

"Either they think I am crazy or they think I am a murderer. That's the way it goes. I wish I had never seen that lousy brother of yours."

"Harvey, you took the Danish out of the air before my brother set foot in the house."

"That's right, I did," said Harvey.

At which moment the Medical Examiner sat facing both Lieutenant Serpio and the Chief of Detectives, and said to them, "It is not a murder because that large blond tomato was never alive."

"I'm a busy man," said the Chief of Detectives. "I have eleven homicides tonight—just tonight on a Sunday night, not to mention two suicides. So don't confuse me."

"I'm confused."

"Good. Now what have you got on that dead blonde?"

"She is only dead in a technical sense. As I said, she was never alive. She is the incredible construction of a bewildered Dr. Frankenstein or some kind of nut. Mostly on the outside she is all right, except that whoever put her together forgot her toenails. Inside, she has no heart, no kidneys, no liver, no lungs, no circulatory system, and practically no blood, and what blood she has is not blood, because nothing she has is like what it's supposed to be."

"Then what's inside of her?" Serpio demanded.

"Mostly a sort of crude beefsteak."

"Just what in hell are you talking about?" demanded the Chief of Detectives.

"You got me," said the Medical Examiner.

"Come on, come on, I bring you a dead seven-foot blonde that makes you wish you were a single basketball player even when she's dead, and you tell me she never was alive. I seen many tomatoes that are more dead than alive, but there has to be a time when they're alive."

"Not this one. She hasn't even a proper backbone, so she could not have stood up to save her life, and I think I'll write a paper about her, and if I do I'll get it published in England. You know, it's a funny thing, you can get a paper like that published in England and it commands respect. Not here. By the way, where did you get her?"

"Serpio brought her in."

"Naked?"

"Just like she is," Serpio said. "We found her on the floor, stretched out like a lox, in the apartment of two people whose name is Kepplemen. He's an accountant. I got them upstairs."

"Did you charge them?"

"With what?"

"Absolutely beautiful," said the Medical Examiner.

"You know, you go on with this lousy job for years and nothing really interesting ever comes your way. Now did they say where she came from?"

"This Harvey Kepplemen," Serpio replied, watching the Chief of Detectives, "says he took her out of the air."

"Oh?"

"Serpio, what the hell are you talking about?" from the Chief of Detectives.

"That's what he says. He says he takes prune Danish out of the air, and he got her from the same place."

"Prune Danish?"

"Danish pastry."

"All right," the Chief of Detectives said. "I got to figure you're sane and you're not drunk. If you're insane, you get a rest cure. If you're drunk, you get canned. So bring them both to my office."

"I got to be there," said the Medical Examiner. "I just got to be there."

This time Serpio called Harvey Mr. Kepplemen. "Mr. Kepplemen," he said politely, "the Chief of Detectives wants to see you in his office."

"I'm tired," Suzie complained.

"Just a little longer, and maybe we can clear this up—how about that, Mrs. Kepplemen?"

"I want you to know," Harvey said, "that nothing like this ever happened to me before. I have good references. I have worked for the same firm for sixteen years."

"We know that, Mr. Kepplemen. It won't take long."

A few minutes later they were all gathered in the office of the Chief of Detectives, Harvey and Suzie, Serpio, the Chief of Detectives, and the Medical Examiner. The Chief of Detectives poured coffee.

"Go ahead, Mr. and Mrs. Kepplemen," he said. "You've had a long day." His voice was gentle and comforting. "By the way, I am told that you can take Danish pastry out of the air. I can send out for some, but why do that if you can take it out of the air. Right?"

"Well—"

"Harvey doesn't really like to take things out of the air," Suzie said. "He has a feeling that it's wrong. Isn't that so, Harvey?"

"Well," Harvey said uneasily, "well—I mean that all my life I never had a talent for anything. My mother was Ruth Kepplemen . . ." He hesitated, looking from face to face.

"Go on, Harvey," said the Chief of Detectives. "Whatever you want to tell us."

"Well, she was an artist. I mean she painted lots of pictures, and she kept telling her friends, Harvey hasn't a creative bone in his body—"

"About the Danish, Harvey?"

"Well, Suzie and I were driving through Baltimore—"

"Detective Serpio told me about that. I was thinking that here we all are with coffee, and it's past midnight, and maybe you'd like to reach out into the air and get us some prune Danish."

"You don't believe me?" Harvey said unhappily.

"Let's say, we want to believe you, Harvey."

"That's why we want you to show us, Harvey," said Serpio, "so we can believe you and wind this up."

"Just one moment," the Medical Examiner put in. "Did you ever study biology, Harvey? Physiology? Anatomy?"

Harvey shook his head.

"How come?"

"We kept moving around. I just missed out."

"I see. Come on, now, Harvey, let's have that Danish."

Harvey reached out, two feet in front of his nose, and plucked at the air and emerged with air. His face revealed his confusion and disappointment. He plucked a second time and a third time, and each time his fingers were empty.

"Harvey, try water rolls," Suzie begged him.

He tried water rolls with equal frustration.

"Harvey, concentrate," Suzie pleaded.

He concentrated, and still his fingers were empty.

"Please, Harvey," Suzie begged him, and then when she realized it was all to no end, she turned on the policemen and informed them that it was their fault, and threatened to get a lawyer and to sue them and to do all the other things that people threaten to do when they are in a situation such as Suzie was in.

"Serpio, why don't you have a policeman drive the Kepplemens home?" the Chief of Detectives suggested; and when Serpio and Harvey and Suzie had gone, he turned to the Medical Examiner and said that one thing about being a cop was that if you only kept your health, you would see everything.

"Now I have seen everything," he said, "and tell me, Doc, did you lift any fingerprints off that big tomato downstairs?"

"She hasn't any."

"Oh?"

"That's the way it crumbles," said the Medical Examiner. "Every American boy's dream—seven feet high and a size forty-six bust. How do I write a death certificate for something that was never alive?"

"That's your problem. I keep feeling I should have held those two."

"For what?"

"That's just it. Are you religious, Doc?"

"I sometimes wish I was."

"What I mean is, I keep thinking this is some kind of miracle."

"Everything is, birth, death, getting looped."

"Yeah. Well, make it a Jane Doe DC, and put her in the icebox before the press gets a look. That's all we need."

"Yeah, that's all we need," the Medical Examiner agreed.

Meanwhile, back in the four-room apartment, Suzie was weeping and Harvey was attempting to comfort her by explaining that no matter how much he tried, he would have never gotten the ten-dollar-bill problem completely licked.

"Who cares about the damn bills?"

"What then, kitten?"

"Kitten! All these years, and what do you want but an enormous slobbering seven-foot blonde with a forty-six bust."

"It's just that I never got anything that I really wanted," Harvey tried to explain.

"Not even me?"

"Except you, kitten."

Then they went to bed, and everything was about as good as it could be.

9

The Mind
of God

"How do you feel?" Greenberg asked me.

"Fine. Lousy. Frightened. A little sick, a little stupid, empty in the stomach. Nauseous. I think I could throw up at will. But mostly afraid. Otherwise I'm fine."

"Good."

"Why is it good?"

"Because you're facing yourself fully and acknowledging your sensations. That's very important at this moment. If you told me you were filled with noble resolve and without fear, I would be worried."

"I'm worried," I told him. "Damn worried."

"There's no contract, no commitment that's binding," Zvi Leban said slowly, his cold blue eyes fixed on me. I never saw him as the Nobel Prize winner, the brilliant physicist so often compared to Einstein and Fermi; to me he was an Israeli, the kind I respect but do not particularly like, cold as ice and full of an implacable will that appears to partake of neither courage nor cowardice, only resolution. "The door's open."

"Zvi—stop that," Dr. Goldman said quietly.

"It's all right," said Greenberg. Greenberg was many things, M.D., psychiatrist, physicist, philosopher, business-man—all of it crowded into a fat, easygoing, moonfaced man of sixty-one years who never raised his voice and never lost his temper. "It's quite all right. He has to face everything now, his fears, his hopes, his resolutions, and also the open door. The fact that he can walk out and there will be no recriminations. You understand that, don't you, Scott?"

"I understand it."

"We have no secrets. A project like this would be mean-ingless and immoral if we had secrets from each other. Perhaps it's immoral in any case, but I am afraid I have lost touch with what men call morality. We had our time of soul-searching, seven years of it, and then we came to our decision. The Sabbath of our soul-searching, I may say, and it's done. Finished. You were and are my friend. I brought you into this in the beginning, and then you placed yourself squarely in the center of it. Zvi was against you, which you also know. He thought it should be a Jew. Goldman and I thought otherwise, and Zvi accepted our decision."

"I'd like to close the door," I said. "I would not have come today if I had not made up my mind. I'm going through with it. I told Zvi that I had no hate left. The hate has washed out. I had to be truthful about that. Zvi regards it as a lack of resolution."

"You never married again," said Goldman.

"I don't quite know what that means."

"There's no point to this discussion now," Zvi said. "Scott is going through with it. He's a brave man, and I would like to shake hands with him."

He did so with great formality.

"You've thought of some questions?" Goldman asked. "We still have an hour." He was a thin wisp of a man, his brilliance honed down to knife-edge. He had an inoperable malignancy; in a year he would be dead, yet his impending doom appeared to arouse in him only curiosity and a vague sadness. They were three unusual men indeed.

"Some. Yes, I've thought of some that I haven't asked before. I don't know that I should ask them now."

"You should," said Goldman. "You go with enough doubts. If you can clear up a few of them, so much the better."

"Well, I've been brooding over the mathematics of it, and I still can't make head or tail of them, but I'm afraid an hour's no good for that."

"No."

"Still one tries to translate into images. I suppose the mathematicians never do."

"Some do, some don't," Zvi said, smiling for the first time. "I have, but it impeded my work. So I gave it up. Just as there are no words for things we do not know, so there are no images for concepts outside of our conceptual experience."

"Specifically, Scott?" Greenberg asked me.

"It always comes down to breaking the chain. Then the result is entirely different. For example, this project would not take place. We would not be standing here in a stone warehouse in Norwalk, Connecticut. We would not have planned what we planned. The necessity would not face us."

"Conceivably."

"Then would I take the chance of destroying you—and thousands, perhaps millions of others now alive?"

"There," said Zvi, "is where the conceptual and the mathematical part. The answer is no, but there is no way I can explain."

"Can you explain to yourself?"

Zvi shook his head slowly, and Greenberg said, "No more, Scott, than Einstein could visualize to himself his proposition that space might be curved and limited."

"But I can visualize," I protested. "Nothing as complicated as Einstein's proposition, but I can visualize sending me back twenty-four hours. At this time yesterday, the four of us were here, sitting at this same table. I was drinking a scotch and water. What then? Would there have been two of me, identical?"

"No. It would simply be yesterday."

"And if I had a bottle of wine in my hand instead of a glass of scotch?"

"Then you propose the paradox," Goldman said gently, "and so our powers of reason cease. Which is why we do not test the machine. My dear Scott—you and I both face death, and that too is a paradox and a mystery. We are physicists, mathematicians, scientists, and we have discovered certain coordinates and from them developed certain equations. Our symbols work, but our minds, our vision, our imagination cannot follow the symbols. I may brood over a death that is inevitable, the maturation of a malignancy within me; you, as a far braver man, accept the likelihood of death in your own undertaking. But neither of us can comprehend what faces us. Do you think of yourself as a good Christian?"

"Not particularly."

"Perhaps no more than I think of myself as a good Jew —if indeed either term has any meaning. But long ago I heard the legend of Moses, who could not enter the promised land. Then, standing at his side on Mount Nebo, God revealed to him all that had been and all that would be—the past and the future, all of it existent in God's time. That too is in symbols. Do you understand why we cannot take the chance of testing the machine, of sending you back even a single day?"

"Not really."

"Then you must take our word for it, as you have."

I shrugged and nodded.

"Any other questions, Scott?" Greenberg asked me.

"A thousand—plus all I have asked before. I have the questions, but you have no answers."

"I wish we had them," Goldman said. "I truly do."

"All right, let's get on with it. First, the money."

Greenberg laid it in small piles on the table. "Ten thousand dollars, American. We would have liked it to be more, but we think that this will cover every contingency. Not easy to come by, believe me, Scott. We pulled some of the largest strings we have in Washington, and if anyone tells you museum officials cannot be bribed, he is mistaken. Pay for everything in cash without any trepidation. It was the most common method in those days. There are two hundred pounds British. Just in case."

"In case of what?"

"Who knows? We simply do not wish you to have to exchange money, and thus we include these small sums in francs and lire."

"And in marks?"

"German and Austrian—about five thousand dollars in each. Strangely enough, they were easier to obtain than the dollars. We have our own sources through dealers. Indeed, most of the marks came from one man who had some sense of what we were doing. No hard money; that would only make problems."

"The revolver?"

"We decided against it. We know it was common practice at the time to carry one, but in this case you are safer with only the knife. Here it is." He placed a pearl-handled folding knife on the table. "Four blades, common gentleman's possession at the time. You will use the large one. It's honed to a razor edge."

Zvi watched me carefully, his eyes slitted. I opened the pearl-handled knife and ran my finger along the edge of the blade. I was rather relieved that they had decided against the revolver; after all, it was probably a more civilized world than the one we live in.

Goldman brought a large cardboard box and placed it on the table. "Your clothes," he explained, smiling almost apologetically. "You can begin to change now. Amazing how much in style they are. You may want to keep them afterwards."·

"Afterwards—"

Greenberg waited, his face thoughtful.

"We are afterwards. That's what keeps tearing my gut."

"Get it out, Scott," Greenberg said.

"We are afterwards. That's all."

"Let go of it. Our minds are not made for a paradox."

" 'My ways are not thy ways; neither are my thoughts thy thoughts,' " Goldman said.

"Quoting God?"

Goldman grinned, and suddenly I relaxed and began to peel off my clothes.

"Damn you, I envy you," Zvi said suddenly. "If I did not have this cursed limp and two duodenal ulcers, I would go myself. It's what no man has ever been offered, what no man has ever experienced. You step into the mind of God."

"For atheists, you Jews are the most frantically religious people I have ever known."

"That's also part of the paradox," Greenberg agreed. "The label in the suit is Heffner and Kline. They were excellent custom tailors. Imported Irish tweed, hand spun and hand woven. Your valise contains another suit, dark blue cheviot. Both of them rather heavy for May, but they didn't go in for tropicals in those days. Also six shirts, underclothes, and all the rest."

He brought the valise from where it stood by the wall, next to the strange maze of tubes and wires it had taken them seven years to build. Goldman fitted the collar to the shirt and handed it to me.

"Ever wear one of these?" he inquired.

"My father wore them." It was the first time I had thought about my father in years, and suddenly I was overwhelmed with the memory.

"No." Zvi shook his head.

"Why not?" I asked desperately. "Why not? He wouldn't know me."

"You would not know him either," Zvi said evenly. "It will be eighteen ninety-seven. You were not born until nineteen twenty. How old was he then when you were born?"

"Thirty-six."

"Then in eighteen ninety-seven he would be a boy of thirteen—to what end, Scott?" Greenberg asked.

"I don't know to what end. So help me God, I don't know. But if I could only look at him!"

Goldman walked over to me and helped me adjust the two gold buttons that held the collar to the shirt. "There, now. You will let me tie the cravat, Scott. I know exactly how it should be done. And watch me carefully, so you can do it yourself. And take our word for it. We are interfering with a schematic—a great, enormous schematic —so we must interfere as little as possible. What Zvi said before is quite true—we enter the mind of God. We are bold men, all of us. Also, perhaps, we are madmen—as the people who exploded the first atomic bomb were madmen. They tampered with the mystery, and the world paid a price. We also tamper with the mystery, and we shall also pay a price. But we must tamper as little as possible. You must not be diverted. You must speak to no one unless it is absolutely necessary. You must not touch things, you must not change things—except the single thing to which we are pledged. Now watch how I tie the cravat—very simple, isn't it?"

I had gotten hold of myself now and wanted nothing else than to get on with it. Greenberg helped me into the tweed jacket.

"Beautiful. We have not traduced the tradition of Heffner and Kline. You are a well-dressed, upper-class gentleman, Scott. Now try this hat."

He handed me a soft felt hat, which fitted quite well.

"My grandfather's," he said with pleasure. "By golly, they made things to last, didn't they? Now listen carefully, Scott—we have only ten minutes remaining to us. Here's your wallet." He handed me an oversized, bulging wallet of alligator hide. "Papers, identity, everything you need. Knife, money—change your shoes. These are hand made. Every detail. In the wallet you will find a complete and detailed itinerary, just in case you should forget some detail. This watch"—giving me a magnificent pocket watch with a cover of embossed gold—"belonged to my grandfather. Comes with the hat. Completely overhauled, it keeps perfect time."

I finished buckling on the excellent handmade Victorian boots. Soft as butter, there would be no problem of breaking them in. Greenberg went on with his instructions, precisely, rapidly.

"You have exactly twenty-nine days, four hours, sixteen minutes, and thirty-one seconds. At that time after your arrival, you must be back here in this warehouse and in the same spot. It will then have been abandoned three years, and it should be as empty as when my grandfather bought the property half a century ago. Now in a few minutes I am going to mark your boots with a red pigment that will come off when you step away. No matter how nervous or startled you are upon arrival, a red outline of your boots will remain on the floor. When you return, you step into the same position. Is that clear?"

"Clear."

"You will walk to the railroad station, take the first train to New York, and buy your round-trip steamship passage immediately. From the time you arrive until the SS *Victoria* sails, you have eighteen hours. Spend them on board ship in your cabin. On the voyage, talk to as few people as possible. Plead seasickness, if you will."

"I won't have to plead it."

"Good enough. The ship docks at Hamburg, where you buy a first-class through ticket to Vienna. But of course you know all that, and of course you have detailed written instructions in your wallet. You've brushed up on your German?"

"My German is adequate. You know that. What happens if I don't get back to the warehouse in time?"

Greenberg shrugged. "We don't know."

"I live on in a world where my father is a child?"

"You keep invoking the paradox," said Zvi. "Don't do that. It's hurtful to you, hurtful to your mind."

"My mind's all right," I assured him. "A man with one foot in hell doesn't trouble about his mind. It's my body that worries me."

"Only four minutes," Greenberg said gently. "Would you step over here, Scott. Stand precisely between the electrodes and hold the valise as close to your body as you can."

"Cigars!" I remembered. "Good God, I don't have a cigar on me."

"They were better in those days. Pure Havana. Buy some. Now take your place!"

I grabbed the valise, fixed Greenberg's grandfather's hat

firmly on my head, and stood where I was instructed to stand.

"One foot at a time," said Greenberg, kneeling in front of me. He marked each sole and heel with a dab of heavy red pigment. "Now don't move."

"Three minutes," Goldman said.

"You look damned impressive in that hat and suit," Zvi admitted.

"How long will I be away?" I wanted to know. "I mean in your time. Here. How long do you wait until I return?"

"We don't wait. If you return, you are still here."

"That's insane."

"That's the paradox," said Zvi. "I warned you not to think about it."

"Two minutes," Goldman said.

Zvi put his hand on the switch. Goldman's lips were moving silently. Either he was praying or counting the seconds.

"Suppose something's in the way," I said desperately. "Bales, boxes. How can two objects occupy the same space? What happens to me then?"

"It won't happen. That's also part of the paradox."

"If it's such a goddamn paradox, how can you be so sure? How do you know?"

I was high-strung, frightened, despairing, and losing my nerve. In a few seconds, I would be hurtled back seventy-five years through time—riding on a set of coordinates that had come out of someone's strained logic, on an equation that had never been proved or tested—into hell or the mind of God or nothingness or the Mesozoic age, armed with a pearl-handled pocketknife and an ancient valise.

"One minute," Goldman said.

"Do you want to step out?" Greenberg asked, his voice half a plea. He too was frightened. They all were.

I shook my head angrily.

"Thirty seconds," said Goldman, "twenty, ten, nine, eight, seven, six, five, four, three, two, one, zero—"

I saw Zvi pulling the switch. When I returned, twenty-nine days, four hours, sixteen minutes, and thirty-one seconds later, his hand was still on the switch and I heard the soft vowel sound as Goldman finished saying zero. I stood there and they stood there, in a frozen tableau that appeared to go on and on.

Zvi spoke first. "Where is the valise?"

"For heaven's sake, let him sit down and rest," said Greenberg, helping me to a chair. I was shaking like a leaf. Goldman poured a glass of brandy and held it to my lips, but I shook my head.

"Are you cold?" Goldman asked.

"I'm not in shock. Just frightened. Breathless. I had to run the last hundred yards to the warehouse, and I made it by seconds. I threw the valise away."

"That doesn't matter."

"He failed," Zvi said bleakly. "God almighty, he failed. I knew it."

"Did you fail?" Goldman asked.

"I'll have the brandy now," I said, my hand still shaking as I took the glass.

"Let him tell it all," Greenberg said. "There will be no recriminations, no accusations. Let that be plain, Zvi. Do you understand me?"

"Seven years." There were tears in Zvi's eyes.

"And six million dollars of my money. We both learned something. Tell us, Scott—did you go back?"

I looked at Goldman, the doomed man, the man with the malignancy—and there was the slightest, thinnest smile on his lips, as if he had known all the time.

"Did you go back?"

I drank the brandy, and then I reached into my breast pocket and took out two large black cigars, handing one to Greenberg, the only cigar smoker among them. I bit off the end and lit it, while Greenberg stared at the cigar in his hand. I puffed deeply and told him it was better than anything he'd find today.

"Did you go back?" Greenberg repeated.

"Yes—yes, I went back. I'll tell you. But let me rest a moment, let me think. Let me remember. Jesus Christ, let me remember!"

"Of course," said Goldman, "you must remember. Relax, Scott. It will come back." He knew already, this withered man who was visited nightly by the Jewish angel of death. He needed no coordinates or equations; he had touched God briefly, as I had, and he knew all the terror and wonder of it. "You see," he explained to Zvi and Greenberg, "he has to remember. You will understand that in a few minutes. But he must have the time to remember."

Greenberg poured me another brandy. He didn't light his cigar. He kept looking at it and handling it. "Fresh," he muttered, sniffing at it. "Very dark. They must have cured the leaves differently."

"I went back," I said finally. "Seventy-five years. It all worked, your machine, your equations, your bloody coordinates. It all worked. It was like being sick for a few minutes—a terrible sense of being sick. I thought I was going to die. And then I was alone in the warehouse, holding my valise, standing right there. Only—" I paused and looked at Goldman.

"Only you could not remember," Goldman said.

"How do you know?"

"What the devil do you mean?" Zvi demanded. "What do you mean, he couldn't remember?"

"Let him tell it."

"I had no memory," I said. "I did not know who I was. or where I was."

"Go on."

"It's not that simple. Do you know what it is to have no memory, absolutely none, to be standing in a place and not know who you are or how you got there? It's the most terrifying experience I have ever known—even worse than the fear I felt when I stepped into that damn machine."

"Could you read, write, speak?" Greenberg asked.

"Yes, I could read and write. I could speak."

"Different centers of the brain," said Goldman.

"What did you do?"

"I put down the valise and paced back and forth. I was shaking—the way I am shaking now. It took a while. I had a rotten headache, but after a few minutes the pain eased. Then I took out my wallet."

"You knew what it was? You knew it was a wallet?"

"I knew that. I knew I was a man. I knew I was wearing shoes. I knew those things. As a matter of fact, I knew a great deal. I hadn't become an imbecile. I was simply without a memory. I was alive and aware of today, but there was no yesterday. So I took out the wallet and went through it. I learned my name. Not my own name, but the name you gave me for the journey. I read the instructions, the timetable, the minute directions you wrote out for my journey, the warning that I must return to the exact spot in the warehouse at a specific time. And the strange thing was that never for a moment did I doubt the instructions. Somehow I accepted the necessity, and I knew that I must do the things that were written down for me to do."

"And you did them?" Greenberg asked.

"Yes."

"With no troubles—no interferences?"

"No. You see, I knew no other time than eighteen

ninety-seven. There I was. Everything was perfectly natural. I could remember no other time, no other place. I
walked to the railroad station, and believe me, Norwalk
Station was an elegant place in those times. The station-
master sold me a ticket on the parlor car. Can you imagine
a parlor car on the New York, New Haven and Hartford
Railroad? And for less than two dollars."

"How did you know where to walk?" Zvi demanded.

"He asked directions," said Goldman.

"Yes, I asked directions. I had no memory, but I was all
right, I was at home there. I booked first-class passage on
the ship to Hamburg—I spent a few hours wandering
around New York." I closed my eyes and remembered
it. "Wonderful, wonderful place."

"And you could function like that?" Greenberg asked.
"It did not upset you that you had no memory?"

"After a while—no. I simply took it for granted. You
see, I didn't know what memory was. A color-blind man
doesn't know what color is. A deaf man doesn't know what
sound is. I didn't know what memory was. Yes, people
spoke about it and that was somewhat bothersome—where
did I go to school, where was I born, questions like that
I avoided because my instructions were to be private. There
were some questions—well, I ignored them. It was a good-
sized ship, very well appointed. I could be by myself."

"Hamburg," Greenberg reminded me.

"Yes. There were no incidents that are important now.
If you want me to tell you how it was then, how places
were, how people were?"

"Later. There will be time for that later. You took the
train for Vienna?"

"Within hours. I followed my instructions and left the
train at Linz, but there was an error there. It was midnight, and I had to wait until nine the following morning

to catch the train to Braunau. I was at Braunau four hours later."

"And then?"

I looked from face to face, three tired, aging Jews whose memories were filled with the pain and suffering of the ages, who had spent seven years and six million dollars to enter the mind of God and change it.

"And then my instructions ended. You know what I suffered and what my wife suffered at the hands of the Nazis. But you had not written down that I was to seek out an eight-year-old boy whose name was Adolf Hitler and that I was to cut his throat with the razor-sharp blade of my pearl-handled knife. You trusted me to remember what was the purpose of our whole task—and I had no memory of what you had suffered or what I had suffered, no memory of why I was there in Braunau. I spent a day there, and then I returned."

There was a long silence after that. Even Zvi was silent, standing with his eyes closed, his fists clenched. Then Goldman said gently:

"We have not thanked Scott. I thank you for all of us."

Still silence.

"Because we should have known," Goldman said. "Do you remember God's promise—that no man should look into the future and know the time of his own death? When we sent Scott back, the future closed to him, and all his memories were in the future. How could he remember what had not yet been?"

"We could try again," Zvi whispered.

"And we would fail again." Goldman nodded. "We are children pecking at the unknown. Because whatever has been has been. I will show you. Scott," he asked me, "do you remember where you dropped the valise?"

"Yes—yes. It was only a moment ago."

"It was seventy-five years ago. How far from here?"

"At the edge of the road at the bottom of the hill."

Goldman picked up a coal shovel that stood by an old coal stove in the corner of the warehouse and he led the way outside. We knew what he was about and we followed him, through the door and down the hill. It was late afternoon now, the spring sun setting across the Connecticut hills, the air cool and clean.

"Where, Scott?"

I found the spot easily enough, took the coal shovel from the frail man, and began to dig. Six or seven inches of dead leaves, then the soft loam, then the dirt, and finally the rotting edge of the valise. It came out in pieces, disintegrating leather, a few shreds of shirts and underwear, rotten and crumbling under my fingers.

"It happened," Goldman said. "The mind of God? We don't even know our own minds. There is nothing in the past we can change. In the future? Perhaps we can change the future—a little."

10

UFO

"You never read in bed," Mr. Nutley said to his wife.

"I used to, you remember," Mrs. Nutley replied. "But then I found it was sufficient simply to lie here and compose my thoughts. To get my head together, as the kids say."

"I envy you. You never have any trouble sleeping."

"Oh, I do. At times. To be perfectly honest," she added, "I think women fuss less than men."

"I don't fuss about it," Mr. Nutley protested, putting aside his copy of *The New Yorker* magazine and switching off his bedside light. "I just find it damned unpleasant. I'm not an insomniac. I just get a notion and it keeps running around in my head."

"Do you have a notion tonight?"

"I find Ralph Thompson a pain in the ass, if you can call that a notion."

"That's certainly not enough to keep you awake. I must

say I've always found him pleasant enough—for a neighbor. We could do worse, you know."

"I suppose so."

"Why are you so provoked about him?" Mrs. Nutley asked, pulling the covers closer to her chin against the chill of the bedroom.

"Because I never know whether he's putting me on or not. I find writers and artists insufferable, and he's the most insufferable of the lot. The fact that I drag my butt into the city every day and do an honest day's work makes me what he refers to as a member of the Establishment and an object of what I am certain he regards as his sense of humor."

"Well, you are upset," said Mrs. Nutley.

"I am not upset. Why is it that I must wait at least an hour before I can think of the proper witty rejoinder to the needling of a horse's ass?"

"Because you are a thoughtful and honest person, and I am thankful that you are. What did he say?"

"The way he said it," Mr. Nutley replied. "A kind of a cross between a leer and a snicker. He said he saw a flying saucer come sailing out of the sunset and settle down in the little valley across the hill."

"Indeed! That isn't even witty. You probably fell into his trap and insisted that there was no such thing as a flying saucer."

"I am going to sleep," said Mr. Nutley. He turned over, stretched, wriggled into the bedclothes, and relapsed into silence. After a minute or so he asked Mrs. Nutley whether she was still awake.

"Quite awake."

"Well, I said to him, why didn't you go down there and look at it if you knew where it landed? He told me he doesn't trespass on millionaires' property."

"Does he really think we're millionaires?"

"A man who sees flying saucers can think anything. What's got into this country? No one saw flying saucers when I was a kid. No one was mugged when I was a kid. No one took dope when I was a kid. I put it to you—did you ever hear of a flying saucer when you were a kid?"

"Maybe there were no flying saucers when we were kids," Mrs. Nutley suggested.

"Of course there weren't."

"No. I mean that perhaps there were none then, but there are now."

"Nonsense."

"Well, it doesn't have to be nonsense," Mrs. Nutley said gently. "All sorts of people see them."

"Which proves only that the world is filled with kooks. Tell me something, if there is such a silly thing as a flying saucer, what the devil is it up to?"

"Curiosity."

"Just what does that mean?"

"Well," said Mrs. Nutley, "we are curious, they are curious. Why not?"

"Because that kind of thinking is exactly what's wrong with the world today. Wild guesses with no foundation. Do you know that yesterday the Dow dropped ten points because someone made a wild guess and put it on the tape? If people like yourself were more in touch with the world and what goes on in the world, we'd all be better off."

"What do you mean by people like myself?"

"People who don't know one damn thing about the world as it really is."

"Like myself?" Mrs. Nutley asked gently. She rarely lost her temper.

"Well, what do you do all day out here in the suburbs or exurbs or whatever it is sixty miles from New York?"

"I keep busy," she replied mildly.

"It's just not enough to keep busy." Mr. Nutley was off

on one of his instructive speeches, which, as Mrs. Nutley
reflected, came about once every two weeks, when he had
a particularly bad bout of insomnia. "A person must justify
his existence."

"By making money. You always tell me that we have
enough money."

"I never mentioned money. The point is that when the
kids went away to college and you decided to go back and
get a doctorate in plant biology, I was all for it. Wasn't I?"

"Indeed you were. You were very understanding."

"That's not the point. The point is that two years have
gone by since you got that degree and you do absolutely
nothing about it. You spend your days here and you just
let them slide by."

"Now you're angry at me," said Mrs. Nutley.

"I am not angry."

"I do try to keep busy. I work in the garden. I collect
specimens."

"You have a gardener. I pay him one hundred and ten
dollars a week. You have a cook. You have a maid. I was
reading an article in the *Sunday Observer* about the aim-
less life of the upper-middle-class woman."

"Yes, I read the article," said Mrs. Nutley.

"You never let me get to the point, do you?" Mr. Nutley
said testily. "We were talking about flying saucers, which
you are ready to accept as a fact."

"But now we're talking about something else, aren't we?
You're provoked because I don't find a job in some university as a plant biologist and prove that I have a function
in life. But then we'd never see each other, would we? And
I am fond of you."

"Did I say one word about you getting a job in some
university? As a matter of fact, there are four colleges
within twenty miles of here, any one of which would be
delighted to have you."

"That's a matter of surmise. And I do love my home."

"Then you accept boredom. You accept a dull, senseless existence. You accept—"

"You know you mustn't get worked up at this time of the night," Mrs. Nutley said mildly. "It makes it so much harder for you to get to sleep. Wouldn't you like a nice warm glass of milk?"

"Why do you never let me finish any thought?"

"I think I'll bring you the milk. You know it always lets you sleep."

Mrs. Nutley got out of bed, turned on her bedside light, put on her robe, and went down to the kitchen. There she heated a pan of milk. From a jar in the cupboard she took a tiny packet of Seconal and dropped the powder into a glass. She added the hot milk and stirred. Then she returned to the bedroom. Her husband drank the milk and she watched approvingly.

"You do put magic into hot milk," Mr. Nutley said. "It's not getting to sleep that makes me cranky."

"Of course."

"It's just that I think of you all alone all day out here—"

"But I do love this old place so."

She waited until his breathing became soft and regular. "Poor dear," she said, sighing. She waited ten minutes more. Then she got out of bed, pulled on old denims, walking boots, shirt and sweater, and moved silently down the stairs and out of the house.

She crossed the gardens to the potting shed, the moon so bright that she never had to use the flashlight hooked to her belt. In the potting shed was the rucksack, filled with the plant specimens she had collected and catalogued over the past three weeks. They were so appreciative of the care with which she catalogued each specimen and the way she wrapped them in wet moss and the way she always left the fungi for the very last day, so they would be fresh and pungent, that she would be left with a warm glow that lasted for days. Not that she wasn't paid properly and sufficiently for her work. Mr. Nutley was absolutely right. A person with a skill should be paid for the skill, and she had an old handbag half full of little diamonds nestling in the drawer of her dressing table. Of course, diamonds were as common in their place as pebbles were here, so she had no guilts about being overpaid.

She slung the rucksack onto her shoulders, left the potting shed, and took the path over the hill into the tiny hidden valley behind it, where the flying saucer lay comfortably hidden from the eyes of the cynical doubters. She walked with a long, easy stride for a woman of fifty, but then outdoor work tended to keep her in good condition, and she couldn't help thinking how beneficial it would be for Mr. Nutley if he could only spend his time out of doors in the country instead of in a stuffy city office.

11
Cephes 5

The Third Officer (in training, which meant that he was merely the aide to the regular third officer) walked through the corridor of the great interstellar ship toward the meditation room. Although he had spent four years studying the eleven classes of interstellar ships, the reality was new, awesome, and infinitely more complex—the more so since this was a Class Two ship, entirely self-sustaining and with an indefinite cruising range. Unlike other interstellar ships, it was named not for the planet of its origin but for the planet of its destination, Cephes 5, and like all medical ships, it carried clearance for any port in the galaxy.

He knew how fortunate he was to have been appointed to this ship to complete his training, and at the age of twenty-two he was young and romantic enough to doubt and bless his good fortune constantly.

The ship was only three days out of its last port of call—the port where he had come on board as an officer cadet—and since then he had been occupied constantly with medical examinations, inoculations, briefings, and orientation tours. This was his first free hour, and he very properly sought the meditation room.

It was a long, plain room, with ivory-colored walls and ceiling, and lit by a pleasant golden light. Here and there were stacks of cushions, and perhaps a dozen of the ship's one hundred and twenty crew members were in the room, meditating. Each sat upon one of the thin cushions, legs crossed, body erect, hands folded, eyes cast down in a position that was more or less universal in every planet in the galaxy. The Third Officer selected a pillow and seated himself, crossing his bare legs. He was quite comfortable since he wore only a pair of cotton shorts.

He sought to lose himself in his awareness of himself, as he had learned a long time ago, to still his own wonders and doubts and fears and to immerse himself in the wholeness of the universe, his own self becoming part of an infinitely larger self; yet the process would not work. He was blocked, confused and troubled, his mind shaken and swept from thought to thought, while underneath these rushing thoughts, strange and unpleasant fantasies began to form.

He glanced at the other men and women in the meditation room, but they sat in silence, apparently untroubled by the strange and frightening thoughts that hammered at his mind.

For half an hour or so the Third Officer fought to control his own mind and keep it clear and quiet, then he gave up and left the meditation room; and he realized that he had been in this curious state of mental excitement ever since boarding *Cephes 5*, but had only become fully aware of it when he attempted to meditate.

Deciding that it was simply his own eagerness, his own excitement at being assigned to this great, mysterious interstellar cruiser, he went to one of the viewing rooms, sank into a chair, and pressed the button that raised the screen on outer space. The impression was of sitting in the midst of the galaxy, facing a blazing and uncountable array of stars. The Third Officer remembered that on his early training trips the viewing room had been a cure for almost any problem of fear or disquiet. Now it failed him, and his thoughts in the viewing room were as disquieting as they had been in the meditation room.

Puzzled and not untroubled, the Third Officer left the viewing room and sought out the ship's Counsellor. He still had four hours of free time left to him before he began his tour of duty in the engine room, and while he had hoped to devote this time to making the acquaintance of other crew members in the off-duty lounge, he decided now that the first order of importance was to learn why the ship filled him with such a sense of chaos and foreboding.

He knocked at the door of the Counsellor's office, and a voice asked him to enter, which he did gingerly, uncertainly, for he had never before gone to a Counsellor on one of the great galactic ships. The Counsellors were legendary throughout the galaxy, for in a manner of speaking they were the highest rank in all of mankind's table of organization—very old, very wise, and gifted in ways that could only fill a cadet of twenty-two years with awe and respect. On interstellar ships they ranked even above the captain, although it was rare indeed that one of them countermanded a captain's order or interfered in any manner with the operation of the ship. Legend had it that some of the Counsellors were more than two hundred years old, and certainly an age of a century and a half was not uncommon.

Now, as the Third Officer entered the small, simply furnished office, an old man in a blue silk robe turned from the desk where he had been writing and nodded at the Third Officer. He was very old indeed, a black man whose skin was as wrinkled and dry as old brown leather and whose pale yellow eyes looked at the Third Officer with pleasant inquiry. Was it true that the Counsellors were telepaths who could read minds as easily as ordinary men heard sound? the Third Officer wondered.

"Quite true," the old man said softly. "Be patient, Third Officer. There are more things for you to learn than you imagine." He pointed to a chair. "Sit down and be comfortable. There are a hundred and twelve years of difference between your age and mine, and while you may think that a matter of little account when you reach my age, it's very impressive at the moment, isn't it?"

The Third Officer nodded.

"And you were in the meditation room and you found that you could not meditate?"

"Yes, sir."

"Do you know why?"

"No, sir."

"And neither do you suspect why?"

"I have been on spaceships before," the Third Officer said.

"And you have been on this one for three days, and you have been examined, lectured to, shot full of a variety of serums and antibodies, and oriented—but never told what cargo this ship carries?"

"No, sir."

"Or its purpose?"

"No, sir."

"And quite properly, you did not ask."

"No, sir, I did not ask."

The Counsellor regarded the Third Officer in silence for perhaps two or three minutes. The Third Officer by now found his own problems submerged in his excitement and curiosity at actually sitting face to face with one of the fabled Counsellors, and finally he could contain himself no longer.

"Would you forgive me if I ask a personal question, sir?"

"I can't imagine any question that requires forgiveness," the Counsellor replied, smiling.

"Are you reading my mind now, sir? That's the question."

"Reading your mind now? Oh, no—no indeed. Why should I? I know all about you. We need unusual young men in our crew, and you are quite an unusual young man. Reading your mind would take great concentration and effort; quite to the contrary, I was looking into my own mind and remembering when I was your age. But that's a problem of the aged. We tend to be too reflective and to wander a good deal. Now concerning the meditation—it will take a little time, but once you fully understand the purpose of *Cephes 5*, you will overcome these disturbances and indeed you will find that you meditate on a higher level than before—commensurate with a new effort of will. Let that be for a moment. Do you know what the word *murder* means?"

"No, sir."

"Have you ever heard it before?"

"No, sir. Not that I remember."

The old man appeared to be smiling inwardly, and again there was a minute or two of inner reflection. The Third Officer waited.

"There is a whole spectrum of being that we must examine," the Counsellor said finally, "and thus we will introduce you to an area of being you have possibly never dreamed of. It won't damage you or even shake you overmuch, for it was taken into consideration when you were chosen to be a part of the crew of *Cephes 5*. We begin with murder as an idea and an act. Murder is the act of taking a human life, and as an idea it has its origin in abnormal feelings of hatred and aggression."

"Hatred and aggression," the Third Officer repeated slowly.

"Do you follow me? Do you understand?"

"I think so."

"The words are possibly unfamiliar. Allow me to go into your mind for just a moment—and you will feel this better than I could explain it."

The old man's face became blank, and suddenly the Third Officer winced and cried out in disgust. The old black man's face became alive again, and the Third Officer put his face in his hands and sat that way for a moment, shivering.

"I'm sorry, but it was necessary," the Counsellor said. "Fear is very much a part of it, and that is why I had to touch the fear and horror centers of your mind. Otherwise, how do you explain color to a blind man?"

The Third Officer looked up and nodded.

"You will be all right in a moment. Murder is the act— the finality of what you just felt. There are other degrees, pain, torture, an incredible variety of hurts—tell me if any of these words elude you."

"Torture, I don't think I ever heard the word."

"It's a deliberate inflicting of pain, psychological pain, physical pain."

"For what reason?" the Third Officer asked.

"There you have the crux of it. For what reason? Reason implies health. This is sickness, the most dreadful sickness that man has ever experienced."

"And murder? Is it simply a syndrome? Is it something out of the past? Out of the childhood of the races of mankind? Or is it a postulate?"

"No indeed. It's a reality."

"You mean people kill other people?"

"Exactly."

"Without reason?"

"Without reason as you understand reason. But within the spectrum of this sickness, there is subjective reason and cause."

"Enough to take a human life?" the Third Officer whispered.

"Enough to take a human life."

The young man shook his head. "Incredible—just incredible. But consider, sir, with all due respect, I've had an education, a very good education. I read books. I watch television. I have kept myself informed. How can it be that I've never heard of this—indeed that I've never even heard the words?"

"How many inhabited planets are there in the galaxy?" the old man asked, smiling slightly.

"Thirty-three thousand, four hundred and sixty-nine."

"Seventy-two, since Philbus 7, 8, and 9 were settled last month. Thirty-three thousand, four hundred and seventy-two. Does that answer your question? There are thousands of planets where murder has never occurred, even as there are thousands of planets that have never known tuberculosis, or pneumonia or scarlet fever."

"But we heal these things—and almost every other disease known to man," the Third Officer protested.

"Yes, almost every other disease. Almost. We have no knowledge that is absolute. We learn a great deal, but the more we know, the wider the boundaries of the unknown become, and the one disease that defeats our wisest physicians and researchers is this thing we are discussing."

"Has it a name?"

"It has. It is called insanity."

"And you say it's a very old disease?"

"Very old."

It was the Third Officer's turn to be thoughtful, and the old man waited patiently for him to think it through. Finally the cadet asked, "If we have no cure, what happens to these people who murder?"

"We isolate them."

Realization came to the Third Officer like a cold chill. "On the planet Cephes 5?"

"Yes. We isolate them on the planet Cephes 5. We do it as mercifully, as kindly as we can. Long, long ago other alternatives were tried, but they all failed, and finally they came to the conclusion that only isolation would work."

"And this ship—" The Third Officer's voice trailed away.

"Yes—yes, indeed. This is the transport ship. We pick up these people in every part of the galaxy and we take them to Cephes 5. That is why we choose our crew with such care and concern, people of great inner strength. Do you understand now why your meditation went so poorly?"

"Yes, I think I do."

"No sensitive person can escape the vibrations that fill this ship, but you can learn to live with them and deal with them, and find new strength in the process. Of course, you always have the option of leaving the ship."

The old black man looked at the Third Officer thoughtfully, thinking rather wistfully of the precious, fleeting beauty of youth, the unfaded golden hair, the clear blue eyes, the earnest facing and assumption of the problem of life, and he remembered the time when he had been young and strong-limbed and beautiful, not with regret, but with the apparently eternal fascination in the life process that was a part of his being.

"I don't think I will leave the ship, sir," the Third Officer said after a moment.

"I didn't think you would." The Counsellor rose then, standing tall and straight and lean, his blue robe hanging from his bony shoulders, his great height and wide shoul-

ders a quality of the black people on the Rebus and Alma
constellation of planets. "Come now," he said to the boy,
"we will go into this somewhat more fully. And remember,
Third Officer, that we have no alternatives. This is a ge-
netic factor in these poor souls, and had we not isolated
them in this fashion, the whole galaxy would be infected."

The Third Officer opened the door for him and then
followed the Counsellor down the corridor to one of the
elevators. They passed other crew members on the way,
men and women, black and white and yellow and brown
people, and each of them made a gesture of respect to the
Counsellor. They paused at the elevators, and when a door
opened, they stepped in. The Captain of the ship was just
leaving the elevator, and she held the door for a moment
to tell the Counsellor that he looked well and rested.

"Thank you, Captain. This is Third Officer Cadet. He
is with us only three days."

The Third Officer had not seen the Captain before, and
he was struck by the grace and beauty of the woman. She
appeared to be in her middle fifties, yellow-skinned with
black slanting eyes and black hair hardly touched with
gray. She wore a white silk robe of command, and she
greeted the Third Officer graciously and warmly, giving
him the feeling of being vitally needed and important.

"We were discussing Cephes 5," the Counsellor explained. "I take him now to the sleep chamber."

"He is in good hands," the Captain said.

The elevator dropped into the bowels of the great space-
ship, stopped, and the door opened. The Third Officer
followed the Counsellor out into a long, wide chamber
that at first glance left him breathless and shaken—a place
like a great morgue where on triple tiers of beds at least
five hundred human beings lay asleep, men and women
and children too, some as young as ten or twelve years,
none much older than their twenties, people of every race

in the galaxy. In their sleep, there was nothing to distinguish them from normal people.

The Third Officer found himself whispering. "That's not necessary," the Counsellor said. "They cannot awake until we awaken them."

The old man led the young man down the long line of beds to the end of the chamber, where, behind a glass wall, men and women in white smocks were working around a table on which a man lay. A network of wires was attached to a band around his skull, and in the background there were banks of machines.

"We block their memories," the Counsellor explained. "That we are able to do, and then we build up a new set of memories. It's a very complex procedure. They will have no recollection of any existence before Cephes 5, and they will be fully oriented toward Cephes 5 and the mores there."

"Do you just leave them there?"

"Oh, no—no indeed. We have our agencies on Cephes 5; we have maintained them there for many, many years. Feeding these people into the life of Cephes 5 is a most delicate and important process. If the inhabitants of Cephes 5 were to discover this, the consequences for them would be tragic indeed. But there is very small chance of that. Indeed, it is almost impossible."

"Why?"

"Because the entire pattern of life on Cephes 5 depends on ego structure. Every person on the planet spends his life creating an ego structure which subjectively places him at the center of the universe. This ego structure is central to the disease, for given the sickness that creates the ego, each individual goes on to form in his mind an anthropomorphic superman whom he calls God and who supports his right to kill."

"I am not sure I understand," the Third Officer said.

"In time you will. It is enough to accept the fact that the people on Cephes 5 place their planet and their own selves at the center of the universe, and then they structure their lives so that no uncertainty concerning this should ever arise. This is why we have been able to continue this process for so many years. You see, they refuse to even consider the fact that mankind might exist elsewhere in the universe."

"Then they don't know?"

"No, they don't know."

For a while they stood there, the Third Officer watching the work on the other side of the glass panel and growing more and more uneasy. Then the Counsellor tapped his shoulder and said, "Enough. Even in their sleep, they think and dream, and you are still too new to this to suffer their vibrations for long. Come, we will go to one of the viewing rooms, sit and look at the universe, and talk a little more and compose ourselves."

In the viewing room, with the enormous, blazing glory of the stars in front of him and with the comforting presence of the Counsellor beside him, the Third Officer was able to relax and begin to deal with the flood of ideas and impressions. He found that he was full of a great pity, an overwhelming sense of sadness, and he spoke of this to the old man.

"It's quite normal," the Counsellor said.

"What do they do on Cephes 5?" he wondered.

"They kill."

"Then is the planet empty?"

"Hardly. You see, these poor demented creatures are aware of their function, which is to kill, and like all creatures with a sense of function, they place the function above all else. Thus they breed like no other men in the universe, increasing their population constantly, so that while their killing mounts, their breeding remains ahead of it."

"Are they normally intelligent?"

"Very intelligent—yet their intelligence is to no effect. Their egos prevent them from ever turning it inward."

"But how can they be intelligent and continue this thing you call murder?"

"Because the intelligence is directed toward only one end—the killing of their own kind. As I told you, they are insane."

"But if they are intelligent, won't they devise ways to move through space?"

"Oh, yes. They have done so, with very crude rockets. But we chose Cephes 5 originally because it is the farthest inhabitable planet from the center of the galaxy, almost forty light-years from another inhabitable planet. They will move through space, but the problem of warping space, of moving faster than light—this will always elude them, for this is a problem that man can solve only within himself."

For some time the Third Officer sat in silence, and then he asked softly, "Do they suffer a great deal?"

"I am afraid so."

"Is there any hope for them?"

"There is always hope," the old man replied.

"We call it Cephes 5 in our table of planets," the Third Officer said. "But every planet has a subjective name for itself. What do these people call their planet?"

"They call it the Earth," the old man said.

12
The Pragmatic Seed

Four, five, six billion years ago the seed drifted through space. Then the seed was simply a seed, and it had no knowledge of itself. It rode the electronic and magnetic winds of the universe, and neither time nor space existed for the seed. It was all chance, for the seed had absolutely no idea of what it required or what its ultimate destiny was. It moved through a starry, incredible universe, but it also moved through empty space, for the stars and the galaxies were only pinpoints of illumination in infinity.

The professor and the priest were old, good friends, which made their talks easy and not terribly argumentative. The one taught physics, the other taught religion. They were both in their middle years, beyond most passions, and they savored simple things. On this particular fall day, they met after an early dinner and strolled across the campus. It was a cool, delightful October evening, the sun still an hour before setting, the great maples and oaks robed in marvelous rust and amber—as the priest remarked, an evening to renew one's faith.

"I had always thought," said the professor, "that faith was an absolute."

"Not at all."

"How can it be otherwise? Of course," the professor added, "I speak as a man of little faith."

"More's the pity."

"But some little knowledge."

"I am glad you qualify it."

"Thank you. But aren't we both in the same boat? If your faith needs periodic renewing, and can be influenced by so commonplace an event as the action of certain chemicals in the leaves of deciduous trees, then it is as relative as my small store of knowledge."

Lost in his thoughts for a minute or so, the priest admitted that the professor raised an interesting point. "However," he said, "it is not my faith but myself that wants renewing. Just as God is absolute, so is my faith absolute."

"But God, if you choose to believe in Him, is not knowable. Is your faith also unknowable?"

"Perhaps—in a manner of speaking."

"Then thank heavens science does not depend on faith. If it did, we should all be back in the horse-and-buggy era."

"Which might not be the worst thing in the world," the priest speculated.

In the infinity of space, however, the laws of time and chance cease to exist, and in a million or a billion years—one being as meaningless as the other—the winds of space carried the seed toward a galaxy, a great pinwheel of countless blazing stars. At a certain point in space, the galaxy exerted its gravitational pull upon the seed, and the seed plunged through space toward the outer edge of the galaxy. Closer and closer it drove, until at last it approached one of the elongated arms of the pinwheel, and there it was trapped in the gravitational field of one of the countless stars that composed the galaxy. Blindly obedient to the laws of the universe, the seed swung in a great circle around the star, as did other bits of flotsam and jetsam that had wandered into the gravitational field of the star. Yet while they were all similarly obedient to the laws of chance, the seed was different. The seed was alive.

"No, it might not be the worst thing in the world," the professor admitted, "but as one who has just recovered from an infection that might well have killed him had it not been for penicillin, I have a bias toward science."

"Understandably."

"And some mistrust of a faith that renews itself with the beauty of a sunset." He pointed toward the wild display of color in the west.

"Nevertheless," the priest said gently, "faith is more constant and reliable than science. You will admit that?"

"By no means."

"Surely you must. Science is both pragmatic and empirical."

"Naturally. We experiment, we observe, and we note the results. What else could it be if not pragmatic and empirical? The trouble with faith is that it is neither pragmatic nor empirical."

"That's not the trouble with faith," said the priest. "That's the basis of faith."

"You've lost me again," the professor said hopelessly.

"Then you get lost too easily. Let me give you an example that your scientific mind can deal with. You've read St. Augustine?"

"I have."

"And if I say that the core of my faith is not very different from the core of St. Augustine's faith, you would accept that, would you not?"

"Yes, I think so."

"You have also read, I am sure, the *Almagest* of Claudius Ptolemy, which established the earth as the center of the universe."

"Hardly science!" the professor snorted.

"Not at all, not at all. Very good science, until Copernicus overturned it and disproved it. You see, my dear friend, empirical knowledge is always certain and absolute, until some other knowledge comes along and disproves it. When man postulated, thousands of years ago, that the earth was flat, he had the evidence of his own eyes to back him up. His knowledge was certain and provable, until new knowledge came along that was equally certain and provable."

"Surely more certain and provable. Even your fine Jesuit mind must accept that."

"I am a Paulist, if it matters, but I accept your correction. More provable. More certain. And vastly different from the earlier theory. However, the faith of St. Augustine can still sustain me."

The life within the seed and the structure of that life gave it a special relationship to the flood of light and energy that poured out of the star. It absorbed the radiation and turned it into food, and with food it grew. For thousands and thousands of years the seed circled the star and drank in its endless flood of radiation, and for thousands and thousands of years the seed grew. The seed became a fruit, a plant, a being, an animal, an entity, or perhaps simply a fruit—since all of these words are descriptive of things vastly different from the thing that grew out of the seed.

The professor sighed and shook his head. "If you tell me that a belief in angels has not been shattered, then you remind me of the man who grew wolfsbane to keep vampires off his place. He was eminently successful."

"That's hitting pretty low, for a man of science."

"My dear fellow, you can still maintain the faith of St. Augustine because it requires neither experiment, observation, nor a catalogue of results."

"I think it does," the priest said, almost apologetically.

"Such experiments perhaps as walking in this lovely twilight and feeling faith renewed?"

"Perhaps. But tell me—is medicine, that is, the practice of medicine, empirical?"

"Far less so than once."

"And a hundred years ago? Was medicine empirical then?"

"Of course, when you talk of medicine," the professor said, "and label it empirical, the word becomes almost synonymous with quackery. Obviously because human lives are at stake."

"Obviously. And when you fellows experiment with atomic bombs and plasma and one or two other delicacies, no human lives are at stake."

"We are even. Touché."

"But a hundred years ago, the physician would be just as certain of his craft and cures as the physician today. Who was that chap who removed the large intestine from half a hundred of his patients because he was convinced that it was the cause of aging?"

"Of course science progresses."

"If you call it progress," the priest said. "But you chaps

build your castles of knowledge on very wet sand indeed. I can't help thinking that my faith rests on a firmer foundation."

"What foundation?"

The shape of the thing that the seed became was a sphere, an enormous sphere, twenty-five thousand miles in circumference, in human terms; but a very insignificant sphere in terms of the universe. It was the third mass of matter, counting out from the star, and in shape not unlike the others. It lived, it grew, it became conscious of itself, not quite as we know consciousness, but nevertheless conscious of itself. In the course of the aeons that it existed, tiny cultures appeared upon its skin, just as tiny organisms thrive upon the skin of man. A wispy aura of oxygen and nitrogen surrounded it and protected its skin from the pinpricks of meteors, but the thing that grew from the seed was indifferent, unaware of the cultures that appeared on and disappeared from its skin. For years eternal, it swam through space, circling the star that fed it and nourished it.

"The wisdom and the love of God," the priest replied. That's a pretty firm foundation. At least it is not subject to alteration every decade or so. Here you fellows were with your Newtonian physics, absolutely certain that you had solved all the secrets of the universe, and then along came Einstein and Fermi and Jeans and the others, and poof—out of the window with all your certainties."

"Not quite with all of them."

"What remains when light can be both a particle and a wave, when the universe can be both bounded and boundless, and when matter has its mirror image, antimatter?"

"At least we learn, we deal with realities—"

"Realities? Come now."

"Oh, yes. The reality changes, our vision is broadened, we do push ahead."

"In the hope that at least your vision will match my faith?" the priest asked, smiling.

The thousands of years became millions and the millions billions, and still the thing that was the seed circled the sun. But now it was ripe and bursting with its fullness. It knew that its time was coming to an end, but it did not resist or protest the eternal cycle of life. Vaguely it knew that its own beginning seed had been flung out of the ripened fruit, and it knew that what had been must occur again in the endless cycle of eternity—that its purpose was to propagate itself: to what end, it neither knew nor speculated. Full to bursting, it let be what must be.

The day was ending. The sun, low on the horizon now, had taken refuge behind a lacework of red and purple and orange clouds, and against this the golden leaves of the trees put to mock the art of the best jewelers. A cool evening wind made a proper finish for a perfect day.

No other words. "What a perfect day," the priest said.

"Now that's odd."

They had come to the edge of the campus, where the mowed, leaf-covered lawns gave way to a cornfield.

"Now that's odd," said the professor, pointing to the cornfield.

"What is odd?"

"That crack over there. I don't remember seeing it yesterday."

The priest's eyes followed the pointing hand of the professor, and sure enough, there was a crack about a yard wide running through the cornfield.

"Quite odd," the priest agreed.

"Evidently an earth fault. I didn't know there were any here."

"It's getting wider, you know," the priest said.

And then it got wider and wider and wider and wider.

13
The Egg

It was fortunate, as everyone acknowledged, that Souvan-167-arc II was in charge of the excavation, for even though he was an archaeologist, second rank, his hobby or side interest was the eccentricities of social thinking in the latter half of the twentieth century. He was not merely a historian, but a man whose curiosity took him down the small bypaths that history had forgotten. Otherwise the egg would not have received the treatment it did.

The dig was in the northern part of a place which in ancient time had been called Ohio, a part of a national entity then known as the United States of America. The nation was of such power that it had survived three atomic fire sweeps before its disintegration, and it was thereby richer in sealed refuges than any other part of the world. As every schoolchild knows, it is only during the past century that we have arrived at any real understanding of the ancient social mores that functioned in the last decades of the previous era. A gap of three thousand years is not

easily overcome, and it is quite natural that the age of
atomic warfare should defy the comprehension of normal
human beings.

Souvan had spent years of research in calculating the
precise place of his dig, and although he never made a
public announcement of the fact, he was not interested
in atomic refuges but in another, forgotten manifestation
of the times. They were times of death, a quantity of death
such as the world had never known before, and therefore
times of great opposition to death—cures, serums, antibodies, and—what was Souvan's particular interest—a
method of freezing.

Souvan was utterly fascinated by this question of freezing. It would appear, so far as he could gather from his
researches, that in the beginning of the latter half of the
twentieth century, great strides had been made in the
quick-freezing of human organs and even of whole animals;
and the simplest of these animals had been thawed and
revived. Certain doctors had conceived the notion of
freezing human beings who were suffering from incurable
diseases, and then maintaining them in cold stasis until
such a date when a cure for the particular disease might
have been discovered. Then, theoretically, they would
have been revived and cured. While the method was available only to the rich, several hundred thousand people had
taken advantage of it—although there was no record of
anyone ever being revived and cured—and whatever centers
had been built for this purpose were destroyed in the fire
storms and in the centuries of barbarism and wilderness
that had followed.

Souvan had, however, found a reference to one such
center, built during the last decade of the atomic age,
deep underground and supposedly with compressors func-
tioning by atomic power. His years of work were now
drawing toward consummation. They had sunk their shaft

one hundred feet into the lava-like wasteland that lay south of the lake, and they had reached the broken ruins of what was certainly the installation they sought. They had cut into the ancient building, and now, armed with powerful beacons, laser-cutters, and plain pickaxes, Souvan and the students who had assisted him were moving through the ruin, from hall to hall, room to room.

His research and expectations had not played him false. The place was precisely what he had expected it to be, an institution for the freezing and preservation of human beings.

They entered chamber after chamber where the refrigeration caskets lay row upon row, like the Christian catacombs of a barely remembered past, but the power that drove the compressors had failed three millenniums ago and even the skeletons in the bottom of the caskets had crumbled to dust.

"So goes man's dream of immortality," Souvan thought to himself, wondering who these poor devils had been and what their last thoughts were as they lay down to be frozen, defying that most elusive of all things in the universe, time itself. His students were chattering with excitement, and while Souvan knew that this would be hailed as one of the most important and exciting discoveries of his time, he was nevertheless deeply disappointed. Somewhere, somehow, he had hoped to find a well-preserved body, and with the aid of their medicine, compared to which the medicine of the twentieth century was rather primitive, restore it to life and thereby gain at firsthand an account of those mysterious decades when the human race, in a worldwide fit of insanity, had turned upon itself and destroyed not only 99 percent of mankind but every form of animal and bird life that existed. Only the most fragmentary records of those forms of life had survived, and so much less of the birds than of the animals that those airy, wonderful creatures that rode the winds of heaven were much more the substance of myth than of fact.

But to find a man or a woman—one articulate being who might shed light upon the origin of the fire storms that the nations of mankind had loosed upon each other —that was Souvan's cherished dream, now shattered. Here and there important parts of skeletons remained intact, a skull with marvelous restoration work on the teeth—Souvan was in awe of the technical proficiency of these ancient men—a femur, a foot, and in one casket, strangely enough, a mummified arm. All this was fascinating and important, but of absolutely no consequence compared to the possibilities inherent in his shattered dream.

Yet Souvan was thorough. He led his students through the ruins, and they missed nothing. Over twelve hundred caskets were examined, and all of them yielded nothing but the dust of time and death. But the very fact that this installation had been constructed so deep underground suggested that it had been built during the latter part of the atomic age. Surely the scientists of that time would have realized the vulnerability of electric power that did not have an atomic source, and unless the historians were mistaken, atomic power was already in use for the production of electricity. But what kind of atomic power? How long could it function? And where had their power plant been located? Did they use water as a cooling agent? If so, the power plant would be on the shore of the lake— a shoreline that had been turned into glass and lava. Possibly they had never discovered how to construct a self-contained atomic unit, one that might provide a flow of power for at least five thousand years. It is true that no such plant had ever been found in any of the ruins, but so much of ancient civilization had been destroyed by the fire storms that only fragments of their culture had survived.

At that moment in his musings, he was interrupted by a cry from one of the students assigned to radiation detection.

"We have radiation, sir."

Not at all unusual in a ground-level excavation; most unusual so deep in the earth.

"What count?"

"Point 003—very low."

"All right," Souvan said. "Take the lead and proceed slowly."

There was only one chamber left to examine, a laboratory of sorts. Strange how the bones perished but machinery and equipment survived! Souvan walked behind the radiation detector, the students behind them—all moving very slowly.

"It's atomic power, sir—point 007 now—but still harmless. I think that's the unit, there in the corner, sir."

A very faint hum came from the corner, where a large, sealed unit was connected by cable to a box which was about a foot square. The box, constructed of stainless steel, and still gleaming here and there, emitted an almost inaudible sound.

Souvan turned to another of his students. "Analysis of the sounds, please."

The student opened a case he carried, set it on the floor, adjusted his dials, and read the results. "The unit's a generator," he said with excitement. "Atomic-powered, sealed, rather simple and primitive, but incredible. Not too much power, but the flow is steady. How long has it been since this chamber was last entered?"

"Three thousand years."

"And the box?"

"That poses some problems," the student said. "There appears to be a pump, a circulating system, and perhaps a compressor. The system is in motion, which would indicate refrigeration of some sort. It's a sealed unit, sir."

Souvan touched the box. It was cold, but no colder than other metal objects in the ruins. Well insulated, he thought, marveling again at the technical genius of these ancients. "How much of it," he asked the student, "do you estimate is devoted to the machinery?"

Again the student worked at his dials and studied the fluttering needles of his sound detector. "It's hard to say, sir. If you want a guess, I would say about eighty percent."

"Then if it does contain a frozen object, it's a very small one, isn't it?" Souvan asked, trying to keep his voice from trembling with eagerness.

"A very small one, yes, sir."

Two weeks later Souvan spoke to the people on television. The people were simply the people. With the end of the great atomic fire storms of three thousand years past had come the end of nations and races and tongues. The handful of people who survived gathered together and intermarried among themselves, and out of their tongues came a single language, and in time they spread over the five continents of the earth; and now there were half a billion of them. Once again there were wheatfields, forests and orchards, and fish in the sea. But no song of birds and no cry of any beast; of those, no single one had survived.

"Yet we know something of birds," Souvan said, somewhat awed at speaking for the first time over the worldwide circuit. He had already told them of his calculations, his dig, and his find. "Not a great deal, unfortunately, for no picture or image of a bird survived the fire storms. Yet here and there we were rewarded with a book that mentioned birds, a line of verse, a reference in a novel. We know that their habitat was the air, where they soared on outstretched wings, not as our airplanes fly with the drive of their atomic jets, but as the fish swim, with ease and grace and beauty. We know that some of them were small, some quite large, and we know that their wings were covered with downy things called feathers. But what in all truth a bird or a wing or a feather was like, we do not know—except out of the imaginations of our artists who have created so many of their dreams of what birds were.

"Now, in the last room we examined in the strange resurrection place that the ancient people built in America, in the single refrigeration cell that was still operative, we discovered a small ovoid thing which we believe is the egg of a bird. As you know, there has been a dispute among naturalists as to whether any warm-blooded creature could reproduce itself through eggs, as insects and fish do, and that dispute has still not been finally resolved. Many scientists of fine reputation believe that the egg of the bird was simply a symbol, a mythological symbol. Others state just as emphatically that the laying of eggs was the means of reproduction among all birds. Perhaps this dispute will finally be resolved.

"In any case, you will now see a picture of the egg."

A small white thing, perhaps an inch in length, appeared upon the television screens, and the people of the earth looked upon it.

"This is the egg. We have taken the greatest of pains in removing it from the refrigeration chamber, and now it rests in an incubator that was constructed for it. We have analyzed every factor that might indicate the proper heat, and now having done what we can do, we must wait and see. We have no idea how long the incubation will take. The machine which was used to freeze it and maintain it was probably the first of its kind ever to be built —perhaps the only one of its kind ever to be built—and certainly its builders planned to freeze the egg for only a very short while, perhaps to test the efficiency of the machine. That a germ of living life remains now, three thousand years later, we can only hope."

But with Souvan it was more than a hope. The egg had been turned over to a committee of naturalists and biologists, but with his privileges as the discoverer, Souvan was allowed to remain on the scene. His friends, his family saw nothing of him; he remained in the laboratory, had his meals there, and slept on a cot he had fixed up for himself. Television cameras, trained on the tiny white objects in its glass incubator, reported to the world on the hour, but Souvan—and the committee of scientists as well—could not tear himself away. He awakened from his sleep to prowl through the silent corridors and look at the egg. When he slept, he dreamed about the egg. He pored over pictures of artists' conceptions of birds, and he recalled ancient legends of metaphysical beings called angels, wondering whether these had not derived from some species of bird.

He was not alone in his fanatical interest. In a world without boundaries, wars, disease, and to a large degree without hatred, nothing in living man's memory as exciting as the discovery of the egg had ever happened. Millions and millions of viewers watched the egg through their televisions; millions of them dreamed of what the egg might become.

And then it happened. Fourteen days had gone by when Souvan was shaken awake by one of the laboratory assistants.

"It's hatching!" she cried. "Come on, Souvan, it's hatching."

In his nightclothes, Souvan raced to the incubator room, where the naturalists and biologists had already gathered about the incubator. Amid the hubbub of their voices, he heard the pleas of the cameramen to allow some space for pictures; but he ignored this as he pushed through to see for himself.

It was happening. The shell of the egg was already cracked, and as he watched, a tiny beak pecked its way free, to be followed by a little ball of downy yellow feathers. His first response was one of intense disappointment; was this then the bird? This tiny shapeless ball of life that stood on two tiny legs, barely able to walk and obviously unable to fly? Then reason and scientific training reassured him that the infant need not resemble the adult, and that the very fact of life emerging from the ancient frozen egg was more miracle than he had ever known in his lifetime.

Now the naturalists and biologists took over. They had already determined, piecing together every fragment of information they possessed and using their own wit as well, that the diet of most birds must have consisted of grubs and insects, and they had all the various possible diets ready—so that they might discover which was most congenial to the tiny yellow fluff. They worked with instinct and prayer, and fortunately they found a diet acceptable to the infant bird before it perished of indigestion.

For the next several weeks the world and Souvan observed the most wonderful thing they had ever experienced, the growth of a little chick into a beautiful yellow songbird. It moved from incubator into a cage and then into a larger cage, and then one day it spread its wings and made its first attempt at flight. Almost half a billion people cheered it, but of this the bird knew nothing. It sang, tentatively at first, and then more and more strongly. It sang its trilling little song, and the world listened with more excitement and interest than it gave to any one of the many great symphony orchestras.

They built a larger cage, a cage thirty feet high and fifty feet long and fifty feet wide, and they set the cage in the midst of a park; and the bird flew and sang and circled the cage like a darting ball of sunlight. By the millions, people came to the park to see the bird with their own eyes. They came across continents, across the broad seas —from the farthest reaches of the world, they came to see the bird.

And perhaps the lives of some of them were changed, even as Souvan's life had been changed. He lived now with dreams and memories of a world that once had been, of a world where these airy, dancing feathered things were a commonplace, where the sky was filled with their darting, swooping, dancing forms. What an unending joy it must have been to live with them! What ecstasy to look at them from one's front door, to watch them, to hear their trilling songs from morning to nightfall! He often went to the park—so often that it interfered with his work—to push his way slowly through the enormous crowds until he was near enough to see the tiny dancing bit of sunlight that had returned to the world from aeons past. And one day, standing there, he looked up at the broad blue reaches of the sky, and then he knew what he must do.

He was a world figure by now, so it was not too difficult for him to get an audience with the council. He stood before the august body of one hundred men and women who managed the business of life on earth, and the chairman, a venerable, white-bearded old man of more than ninety years, said to him:

"We will hear you, Souvan."

He was nervous, uneasy—as who would not be to stand before the council—but he knew what he must say and he forced himself to say it.

"The bird must be set free," Souvan said.

There was silence—minutes of silence—before a woman rose and asked, not unkindly, "Why do you say that, Souvan?"

"Perhaps—perhaps because, without being egotistical, I can claim a special relationship to the bird. In any case, it has entered into my life and my being, and it has given me something I never had before."

"Possibly so with all of us, Souvan."

"Possibly, and then you will know what I feel. The bird has been with us for more than a year now. The naturalists I have discussed this with believe that so small a creature cannot live very long. We live by a rule of love and brotherhood. We give for what we receive. The bird has given us one of the most precious of gifts, a new sense of the wonder of life. All we can give it in return is the blue sky—the place it was meant for. That is why I suggest that the bird should be set free."

Souvan left, and the council talked among themselves, and the next day its decision was announced to the world. The bird would be set free. They gave an explanation simply, using the few words that Souvan had spoken.

Thus there came a day, not too long after this, when half a million people thronged the hills and valleys of the park where the cage was, and half a billion more watched their television screens.

Souvan was close to the cage; he had no need for one of the thousand pairs of binoculars trained upon the cage. He watched as the roof of the cage was rolled back, and then he watched the bird.

It stood upon its perch, singing with all its heart, a torrent of sound from the tiny throat. Then, somehow, it became aware of freedom. It flew, first in the cage, then in circles, mounting higher and higher until it was only a bright flicker of sunshine—and then it was gone.

"Perhaps it will return," someone close by Souvan whispered.

Strangely, he hoped it would not. His eyes were filled with tears, yet he felt a joy and completeness he had never known before.